asylum

MARCUS
LOW

Legend Press Ltd, 107-111 Fleet Street, London, EC4A 2AB
info@legend-paperbooks.co.uk | www.legendpress.co.uk

First published in 2017 by Picador Africa, an imprint of Pan Macmillan
South Africa, Private Bag X19, Northlands, Johannesburg, 2116
www.panmacmillan.co.za

Print ISBN 9781789550344
Ebook ISBN 9781789550337
Set in Times. Printing managed by Jellyfish Solutions Ltd.
Cover design by Steve Marking | www.stevemarking.com

Marcus Low is a Cape Town based writer and public health specialist. His novel *Asylum* was in part inspired by the incarceration of patients with drug-resistant forms of TB in SA in 2008.

Follow Marcus at
www.marcuslow.com
or on Twitter
@MarcusLowx

In memory of Mariaan

The Current

These fish have no eyes
these silver fish that come to me in dreams,
scattering their roe and milt
in the pockets of my brain.

But there's one that comes—
heavy, scarred, silent like the rest,
that simply holds against the current,

closing its dark mouth against
the current, closing and opening
as it holds to the current.

— *Raymond Carver (1938–1988)*

preface

TWO YEARS AFTER ARRIVING at the Pearson quarantine facility for pulmonary nodulosis in the Great Karoo of the Republic of South Africa, Barry Wilbert James started keeping a journal. He had been prompted to do so by psychologist Ms Leanne van Vuuren, who was appointed to counsel him after his attempt to take his own life. Though her prompting was motivated by a belief in the power of narrative psychology, James' journalling would turn out to have both significant literary and historical consequences.

Though there have been other accounts, Mr James' journals have arguably become the most compelling firstperson record of the South African manifestation of the most serious outbreak of an infectious disease since the peak of the HIV epidemic. Others, such as Nattrass and Arendse, have written thorough and compelling histories of the so-called new plague. But their histories are of a general and a more traditional nature. Mr James' journals, by contrast, are intensely personal.

What makes Mr James' writing of particular interest, though, is the obvious literary ambition reflected in the journals. He goes out of his way to present himself as a literary underdog and a reluctant writer, and yet, as various critics have noted, the descriptions of his unusual dreams hint at a literary or aesthetic intention, rather than a simple journalling of experience. As he himself wrote in one of the eight recovered notebooks, now exhibited in a display cabinet in the Museum of the Plague in Beaufort West, 'What do you do when you have all the time in the world and yet no time at all? If you are going to sit staring out the window, you might as well write down what you see.'

However, as journalist Steve Gumede discovered, Mr James had, on at least two occasions prior to his admission to Pearson, submitted entries to short-story competitions. Discoveries like these contradict Mr James' portrayal of himself as an uneducated outsider who unexpectedly flourishes in a makeshift library at a remote quarantine facility. As it turns out, Mr James had in fact completed high school at Bishops, the Diocesan College in Cape Town, and was by all accounts an A student, matriculating near the top of his class.

Although, from a certain point – most likely in December 2022 – Mr James wrote with the express hope of being read, there is no indication that the thought of publication ever crossed his mind. Some critics have argued that his misrepresentation of his past, together with the deliberate plotting of a narrative arc (such as it is), indicates that he is in fact writing to be read by a wider public and that he may have been hoping for the journals to be discovered and published at some point – or at least that he was thinking of them as works of fiction, rather than mere accounts of events in the real world.

Other critics have interpreted the misrepresentations to be indicative of Mr James' complicated psychological state – which is to say that he felt the need to lie to himself rather than to an imagined reader, or at least pretend to himself that he was someone other than the person he actually was.

Of course, as is clear from the journals, Mr James does not hide the fact that he is at times an unreliable narrator. Indeed, in as far as the journals contain a narrative arc, this arc hinges on misrepresentation. The literary power of Mr James' journals lies in the fact that he makes these misrepresentations seem an unavoidable outcome of his experience of the infection. Though far from the full picture, it is not entirely inaccurate to describe Mr James as suffering from a form of denial about the nature and cause of his condition – such denial being quite common in patients diagnosed with serious disease. If not an exact history then, the journals could be read as a meditation on the psychology of illness.

Prompted by Van Vuuren, and by his own admission, we have reason to believe that Mr James wrote about his experience as some form of relief or catharsis. Consider, for example, this passage from a barely legible section of the notebook titled First, 'As much of a nightmare as all the coughing is, one gets used to it. It even becomes a companion of sorts. As if you can cough out the past, cough up everything you've done, all your memories, and get it out of you. Until, one day when it is all out, you have nothing left to do but turn into one of those serene corpses the staff are so determined to clear out as soon as possible.'

It seems likely that the water-damaged first notebook contained more of these relatively direct statements about his state of mind and his understanding of the writing process, although, given the extent of the damage, we can of course not be sure. Some hope remains that new technologies will allow these pages to be deciphered. Some critics have suggested a link between the water damage and the dream Mr James describes in which beer is spilled on some of the notebooks – but there is no evidence to support this.

The only other tantalising fragment from the first half of the first notebook that we still have is the following:

'Coughing fit over, I turned the page and stared out at the parking lot with the hard, red Karoo earth beyond, the scattered assortment of throwaway plants being tugged at by a wind that I knew to be cold and sandy – even though I was indoors. A path wound down from the direction of the highway out of sight beyond a rocky ridge. Halfway toward where the ridge met the sky was the high chain-link fence that was supposed to keep us in. I simply sat and stared at the world beyond the fence and tried to imagine what it would be like to walk up that path, out across the ridge, and then to stand out next to the highway holding out my thumb for a ride.'

Making sense of this passage in isolation is difficult. It is, for example, impossible to know which 'evening' James is referring to and in which of the other journals he had been writing. At the very least, though, it gives a clear indication that he was in fact thinking about getting out, escaping from quarantine, despite his claims to the contrary in notebooks Two and Three.

As an introduction, however, this fragment serves as good as any. His writing style, his evocation of place, and above all his reluctant preoccupation with escape are all there. It contains in microcosm what would be fleshed out in the remaining pages of the first notebook and what remains of the other seven.

Compiling this volume has not been easy. Even though the notebooks are numbered, their lack of chronology is notable. Analysis of the sequence of events and of the writing style does, however, allow us to arrange the entries into at least a plausible chronology. It should be stressed that the entries were likely not written in the order presented here. While we can say with some certainty that the account of his first meeting with Van Vuuren was written many months after the fact (in notebook Six), other events appear to have been written about on the day they happened.

We have taken some artistic licence in opening this anthology with the only loose extract, pages most likely torn from a ninth notebook. As with the fragment quoted above, this one seems to capture something of the essence of Mr James' unique perspective on life as a plague victim.

Only illegible and incomplete sections of Mr James' notebooks have not been reproduced here. The account that follows thus comprises the totality of the legible text as found by Dr J von Hansmeyer.

Von Hansmeyer discovered the notebooks on his return to the Pearson facility in September 2023, three months after the facility was evacuated. He had been resident physician at the facility for the entire time period covered in the journals. After finding the notebooks, Dr Von Hansmeyer mailed them to Ms L Van Vuuren, who had emigrated to the United Kingdom following the closure of the Pearson facility. In March 2021 Van Vuuren graciously donated the notebooks to the Museum of the Plague in Beaufort West where they can still be viewed today.

Neither Dr Von Hansmeyer nor Ms Van Vuuren has given any interviews regarding the journals or their authenticity. Through the work of Gumede, however, we know that all persons named in the notebooks were indeed at the Pearson facility at the time in question. We also know from news reports in June 2023 that the body of a man believed to be that of Jonathan Fox was found in a shallow grave on the farm Donkerspruit near Pearson – a find that corresponds with Mr James' account of Fox's death.

In a few instances, for context and to ground the ethereal quality of what is in effect an internal monologue that straddles the precariousness of what are essentially two worlds – one real and one imaginary – we have, on occasion, included notes in the margins of the text. While some of this marginalia is our own, much of it is drawn from the work of Gumede, Nattrass and Arendse. We also drew heavily on the archives held at the Museum of the Plague. We remain deeply indebted to Mr Albertus Jordaan and colleagues at the museum for their assistance.

fragment

OUTSIDE MY WARD WINDOW the world has died. The dead dirt of the Karoo radiates sunlight. The shrill whine of beetles rises from the hard-baked ground. The insects are incessant. They draw out the long moment before the final eruption that is always delayed for another instant.

Hardly anything grows in the wasteland out there. The torn and scrawny shrubs have the look of litter, litter strapped down to a fuckhard earth. The wind, even the slightest breeze, can stay away for days. Then for long hot afternoons it snatches and tugs at the shrubs. I find myself staring out at these days for hours, hypnotised, seeing – despite my dulled and failing mind – into the heart of some long-dead god of human suffering.

I like to imagine that the wasteland beyond the fence stretches into eternity. That this dilapidated old colonial hospital is the only remaining island of life in all the world, that out there there are no towns or cities, no schools or office parks or shopping malls, no businessmen or politicians, no mothers or girls bursting with youth, just one endless silence.

I thank our dead and absent lord for that rocky ridge, I thank him or her or the Eastern Cape Department of Health or whatever for the fact that we cannot see the highway from our ward windows, for making our imprisonment so close to perfect. In this they have been kind to us, generous and thoughtful even. Nothing would hurt as much as to see families driving by in luxury sedans, farmers in their bakkies, or any other sign of a world that has resolved to go on without us. Our isolation is an act of mercy.

The only way forward is to forget about that world, put all such thoughts aside, to live as if the wasteland stretches all the way to the ocean's deserted beaches, to believe that the apocalypse has come and gone and we alone remain here as if in some pretentious piece of theatre.

We are sick and therefore we are isolated, locked up. We must wait out our days here, and then die – so that the healthy ones, the ones we have forgotten about, may live.

S HE, THE REDHEAD WANTS me to keep a journal. She thinks it would help. She says nobody needs to read it, only me. It would help me placate the things gnawing away inside me. I don't know. Write about how you came to be here, about where you're going, your dreams, she says. Your dreams.

I didn't ask her whether she meant the bad dreams I dream at night, or daydreams of being back in Cape Town, back in the real world. I don't have those kind of dreams any more. We don't kid ourselves here. Once you are infected, there's no going back. I do have the other dreams, though, the ones that sneak up on you like thieves in the dark. They are the only way out of here – in those dreams anything is possible, any horror, any one, any thing, even snow. But you always wake up again. You always return. You always find yourself back here again. Here in this semi-desert, sun beating down, one long day after another.

I guess being here is in itself like a dream. One day you are back there, buying beer at the bottle store, taking the bus home, walking in the shade of tall trees, a free man. Then you open your eyes and you are here. Or maybe you close your eyes and you are here. There was a time when I believed that we may wake up from this nightmare. But, no. Dreams do not last for months. Dreams do not reveal all these grim and grimy details, are not this monotonous.

The real reason she wants me to write about all this is because of what I did. I tried to end the dream. After all, in dreams you never actually hit the ground; in the nanoseconds before impact you are wrenched back, back to where you should be. They don't like that. They do all they can to make the dream last as long as possible. They think there is a point to it. They tell themselves that things will change, that a cure will be found for what ails us. Same old story. Hope, eternal hope.

Anyway, when I came round there were three masked faces hovering over me, a dull 'what's up with this one' look in their eyes. I looked past them, hoping to see angels or gods cracking open the pale sky and swooping down to come pick me up for judgement. There was nothing. Just the faces.

Two of the masks helped me up and half carried me up to the ward, my arms slung over their shoulders, my feet dragging behind through the dust. There were questions about why I passed out, what had happened. I couldn't answer them. It was all a blank. Besides, I was groggy and had no inclination to talk. What does it matter, anyway, what happened? What would it change?

Back in the ward I was given a thick, painful injection. I remember hoping it was morphine, but nothing after that until I woke up again, late-afternoon sunbeams drifting in through the window. Dr Von Hansmeyer standing next to the bed peering down at me.

'What happened to you, Barry?' he asked.

Unlike the others, Von Hansmeyer did not wear a mask. And nobody had ever summoned up the guts to ask him why. Still, his cheeks looked as rosy and healthy as ever, and except for his thinning hair, he could still have been a man of thirty. Maybe he knew something the rest of us didn't.

'I don't know. I don't know what happened,' I said.

Then he examined me, spread-eagled like I was some exotic bird laid out in a museum. He shook his head. He looked me in the eyes and said, 'Get yourself cleaned up and come see me in my office in ten minutes.'

As I swung my legs off the bed a shaft of pain shot through my temples. I felt shaky. I hobbled to the bathroom and considered taking a shower. But there wasn't time. I looked into the mirror. There were streaks of blood on my cheek and on my shirt. I wasn't sure where they had come from.

I washed off what I could in the metal basin. Apart from the throbbing in my head, there was no other pain. And no gaping wound either. Where did all the blood come from? Yet, I didn't really care; whatever happened, happened. For all I know I could have coughed up the blood. I've seen others do it, doubling over and hacking up clumps of blood as thick as wads of phlegm.

When I got to Von Hansmeyer's office he was behind his desk filling in a form, a pair of small, round spectacles perched on his nose. From behind him, the last orange rays of sunlight streamed into the room.

'Close the door behind you,' he said, and took off his glasses. The silence in the room was near perfect, the papers on his desk neatly stacked, the décor modern, not a speck of dust. It was hard to believe we were in a hospital in the Karoo. It could so easily have been a doctor's office in Sandton.

'Let's get down to business then,' he said and, again, looked me straight in the eyes. 'Do you want to die, Barry?'

I shook my head, but to be honest, I might well have wanted to. 'They found you unconscious next to the front entrance. You must have fallen from the second-floor balcony. Or jumped. Do you want to talk about it?'

'No, I don't think so,' I said.

'If you want to die, maybe I can understand that. You see people come in here; some never leave or, when they do, they leave in a body bag. Dead. You know this and I know this,

Barry. But some do beat it and go back to normal lives. You have no reason to believe you are not one of the lucky ones.'

'But how do I know I'm not one of the others? The ones who are carried out in a body bag,' I said.

He looked at me, his head tilted to the side, as if seriously considering my words.

'There is a therapist in town, a Ms Van Vuuren. I'll get her to come see you, tomorrow even. She's helping some of the other patients. Is that in order?'

'Sounds okay,' I said and started to get up. 'Will that be all?'

'Yes,' he said and put his glasses back on.

I went for a shower to wash off the remaining blood. I felt warm and dirty. I had a cut above my left eye – the source of the blood? – and there was an ugly swelling on my cheekbone. My jaw felt as though it had moved a half an inch to the right, but I figured that was just the bruising that made my face feel fucked.

So, clearly, I wasn't really hurt very badly at all, and despite a post-morphine grogginess, when the evening bell rang I went down to the dining hall. So much for ending it all.

I found my table-mates in deep discussion over a nuclear test off the east coast of China. They hardly looked up as I sat down. 'Idiots. Those fucking Chinamen are going to get the world shot to smithereens,' Morris said.

'Oh come on, Morris, it is just a show of power,' Jonathan said, leaning back in his chair. 'I don't see why the whole world is so bloody paranoid. Of course they're not going to use the bomb on actual civilians. They know very well the Yanks can do the same to them.' As he spoke, I caught Jonathan glancing at my face. He didn't say anything.

'Then why show their power at all?' Morris asked. 'And the Japs and the Yanks are certainly not as relaxed about it as you are. One wrong step and we'll have fucking war on our hands. This time we're in a tight spot, a very tight spot. The world is balanced on a knife edge, I tell you.'

'I'm with Morris on this one,' Adams nodded. That was just like Adams. He'd let Morris and Jonathan argue, not say a word, and then at the end of it all pick a side.

Me, I didn't say anything. I couldn't care less about the outside world. Whether or not Japan and China started dropping bombs on each other meant nothing to me. I was never getting out of this hospital, and even less so this country. Yet, for some reason, my three table-mates cared a lot about the things they read in the papers. I guess it kept them busy. At the very least it gave them something to argue about.

For dinner there was cabbage soup with samp and thick slices of days-old bread. My jaw hurt when I tried to chew, so I gave up. I wasn't that hungry anyway.

'What happened to you then, Barry? I heard they found you passed out out front,' Morris asked once the Chinese nuclear crisis had been exhausted. He pulled closer my abandoned tray to help himself to the bread I hadn't eaten. My little accident had hung unspoken over the table throughout the meal, like a dirty family secret.

'Don't bother the poor lad,' said Jonathan, patting me on the back like I was some gangly kid trapped on the playground by a gang of bullies.

'No, it's fine. I can't remember much,' I tried to fob off the question. 'Guess Kagiso's gang must have gotten hold of me.' they laughed and Morris said I should watch out, next thing I knew they'd be trying to make me their bitch. He thought his quip was really funny.

They had been joking about the hospital's two rival gangs for some time. Maybe that was just a way to cope, making light of the depravity around us. I'm not entirely sure why I played along. We heard that one of the younger guys had been raped a few days before. Did we believe it? I think I did, probably still do. People can behave in horrific ways when you give them half a chance.

After dinner we lined up for our meds. They had a counter and a list of names and what pills you were supposed to get. They ticked your name off and watched you swallow. When it was my turn, I tossed the two pills into my mouth and drank down a large, plastic cup of water.

Dugan, the broad-shouldered nurse with a freckled face looked at me with cold eyes, eyes that saw an animal on a chain, not a human being. What's your problem, gabba? I thought. I wondered if he knew about the morphine I had had earlier and whether I should still be getting my meds on top of that. But I didn't like talking to him, so I shut up.

As I turned to leave, he cleared his throat and said, 'Whoa, Barry! Let's see.' He had such a whiney way of talking. I imagined ramming a screwdriver into his guts, then twisting it.

I turned back meekly and opened my mouth.

'Tongue,' he said and leaned over to inspect the inside of my mouth.

I wiggled my tongue and thought of asking him whether my jaw seemed skew to him. 'Show me your hands.' I held my hands out palms up. As if for the first time I noticed the seared skin. Must be from the fall.

'Okay,' he growled and let me go.

Morris once said we were being drugged to keep us passive. The blue pill to fight the bug, the red to keep us from breaking down the fences and marauding through the nearest town like a herd of zombies. Whether that was true or not, I always felt a deep, sandy drowsiness overpower me about a half an hour after taking my meds.

That night, though, I wasn't slipping away into dreamless sleep. Instead I was hunched over the toilet vomiting up the sludge I had had for dinner. It must have been an interaction of the drugs – the morphine and my routine meds. I cursed myself for not telling Dugan about the injection. I guess some foolish part of me still liked to believe I was in the kind of hospital where drug interactions would be picked up ahead of time. But I wasn't. I'm not.

DREAMS. WHAT BLISS TO close your eyes on this carnage, to slip into blackness and be swept away to another world.

I was standing on the platform at a railway station. Salt River maybe, although it looked nothing like the Salt River station from which I had taken so many trains in my previous life. For one, it was snowing. The world white-white, blinding. I watched the snowflakes slowly drifting down onto the tracks and felt a surge of emotion as they hit the cold iron rails and settled there, in drifts, white on black.

Were the long days of Karoo sun and heat over? Had I been granted this final grace, my sins been pardoned? Could it be that I'd be going home?

I could hear the approaching rumble of a train. I looked around. There were people on the platform. Real people, not inmates. People in thick coats and woollen hats. People whose faces I could not see. By my side was the heavy grey suitcase I had been lugging about all day. Its handle had been torn off at one end and hung limply. I wondered how I would manage to carry it.

The train screeched in to the station. The doors slid open with a loud swishing sound. I reached down for my suitcase, but another man was already there. 'No, it's okay,' he said.

'I have to take it now.' He started dragging the suitcase away toward the station building. I wanted to stop him, but I knew the train would be leaving any second.

And then, quite suddenly, I was sitting in the train looking out at the falling snow. I knew then that I was not going home; we were heading in the opposite direction. I was going to an unknown place on a train full of unknown people. And even though I knew I would not be coming back, that the factories that whooshed by were instantly hundreds of kilometres behind us, even though I knew that the train would not deliver us anywhere where we'd want to be, I still felt grateful for the snow, the impossible snow. For it seems to me that even in the most bleak of worlds we'll find something to hold on to… even if that is something as impossible as snow in this god-forsaken wasteland.

When I woke in the cold and quiet of the pre-dawn my white sheets were like a landscape blanketed in snow, a landscape that had burst into my head when I tumbled from that balcony and hit my head. Ammonia, the clean, sanitising smell of ammonia, everywhere. It hung over this white landscape, seeing me off, back into sleep.

Ms Van Vuuren was much younger than I expected. A pallid face maybe a little too round, red hair down to her neck, lean stockinged legs that she kept crossed at all times, and a perfectly shaped nose.

'So I guess you know why I have come to see you, Barry? It is okay if I call you Barry, right?' she asked in a voice that betrayed the faintest hint of a smoking habit.

'I guess you can call me that,' I said.

We were up in the room next to Von Hansmeyer's office, a small dusty space with two chairs, a table and a single window looking out over the back fence.

'Dr Von Hansmeyer tells me you had a fall. Do you want to talk about it, Barry?'

'Not particularly.' I looked past her, out the window. I could see the desert-like veld stretching away beyond the fence.

'He thinks you may have tried to commit suicide.'

'Yeah, well, who knows. Whether I jumped or was pushed doesn't much matter. If I go like that or wait it out up in the ward, it's much the same.'

'I'm sorry to hear you feel that way, Barry. So you're not afraid of dying?' She leaned forward as she spoke, a faint scent of lavender moving with her. She seemed so darn interested in it all. 'For how long have you felt like this?'

I said that I couldn't remember feeling any different.

Come to think of it, now that I write this and read it, there was no way for me to have seen her nose back then, at that initial encounter, since she would surely have been wearing a mask. Still, I seem to remember that at that first meeting she smiled a lot – with those neatly painted lips of hers probably also behind a mask. She'd turn her head and her red hair dropped down, just barely touching her shoulder. She was so sincere I almost felt bad for not caring more about myself… or anything else, for that matter.

Almost, but not quite.

She would allow long silences to pass between us. Then, when she seemed sure I would not answer, she'd allow another question to hang in the air between us. I stared at the table. It was easy to let her questions drift by, to let them slip by without a response.

'You are not the first person to go through this, Barry,' she said after a long silence.

'Fuck. Not the last either,' I said.

She looked at me sternly. 'You don't want to talk to me, do you?'

'What do you care?' I said after the briefest hesitation. 'The doc asked you and now you're here. We're only playing out the scene as it's been scripted. Waiting for the train to leave the station.'

'Well, I'm here, Barry, and I'd like to help you,' she said.

I grunted. I wanted to get back to the ward.

'You don't have to talk to me, Barry. If you can't tell me

about your feelings,' she said, 'then maybe you can try writing them down? Just as a way to get it out. You really need to get it all out sometimes. Just give it a chance. No one can bury everything inside. Write whatever comes into your mind, your past, your thoughts, your dreams.'

Ah, your dreams.

'You realise, of course, that all of us – us in here – are going to die soon? What we need is a priest, not therapy.'

'I'm not planning to save you, Barry. I can't do that. But why not let me see what we can do together to make things a bit better? Worst thing that can happen is that we – you and I – have a chat once a week. Surely that's not so bad?' And then after pausing for emphasis. 'Besides, after what happened yesterday, your *fall*, it's either we chat or they put you under round-the-clock surveillance. And you know that means, don't you, Barry? It essentially means that they will lock you up – there's no delicate way of saying it. They'll lock you up.'

'Really? You'd make them lock me up?'

'No, that's not what I said… But we're all here to keep people alive, Barry. To keep *you* alive. We'll do what we have to do.'

Later, back in the ward, back between the cold, white sheets. How could she know anything about me, if I didn't even know? And even if I did jump off that balcony, what was the difference between that and quietly waiting it out here in the ward, listening to the ceaseless coughing all around me? Why did it matter? There was really nothing to be gained. Not for her, for them – and certainly not for me.

Still, the next morning Von Hansmeyer bulldozed his way into the ward and with a loud 'Barry, my good man!' he put down three notebooks and a clutch of pencils on the foot of the bed.

'I hear you are intent on making a bad impression,' he said, and sighed. 'Oh well, Ms Van Vuuren will be coming in again next week. I expect you to at least make an effort. She's a decent girl. And she knows her business.'

I was sitting up now, still sleepy.

'Come on, get dressed. You cant lie here all day. Pull yourself together,' he said, turning to leave.

As soon as the door clicked shut behind him, I lay back again. I could feel the weight of the notebooks next to me. I thought about the shrink with her red hair and her lean stockinged legs. I wondered whether her visits to this place would eventually break her. Then I wondered whether anyone could go through life not ever having their smile shattered at some point. Poor girl…

And then, as I felt my head sinking deep into the pillow, sleep dragging me back down, I remembered how she had looked at me and how she had said, 'I'm not planning to save you.' For the first time, the thought crossed my mind that I might actually want to be saved.

I WAS SITTING AT the ward window, as I often do these days. I find something deeply calming about just sitting, doing nothing. I feel like a schoolboy again and sleeping on after the alarm has gone. It has that illicit sense of lingering about it. Only thing is that there is nothing chasing me. No class to get to, no waiting teachers, no bell that makes your heart beat faster.

So I sit and look out at the parking lot, the silver-grey chain-link glittering in the sunlight, the path creeping up and across the ridge. Every day I sit for longer and longer, watching the landscape shift, the colours change. It is almost as if I've never seen it before. Every day it is like getting to know an old friend all over again.

I don't suppose it is a particularly good view, as views go. But I've come to know it intimately. I know its moods like that of another person, a roommate perhaps, grey and bleak, the fence cold and hard, or shiny after the rain, the earth turning a deep muddy red, or – as I like it best – wind-swept, dry and the light as blinding as though a nuclear bomb has just been detonated. I like staring into these deep days, where light first obliterates all shade and then gives into it, as if though these days carry within their stark lines and slow rhythms the answers to all the unanswerable questions men might think of asking.

I look at it and it calms something inside me. I think it is the harshness of it that does it, the way the wind scoops up handfuls of dust and tosses them against the baking metal of the weathered fenceposts. It is all so senseless, a mechanical nothingness going about its business, with no care in the world, not giving a damn about its lack of hospitality.

Maybe this deathly business is where the poetry of writing comes from. Getting the notebooks from little Ms Narrative Psychologist wasn't the start of anything; it was a mere progression of the weeks and months I had spent peering at that gaping hole in the fabric of things. The notebooks, these notebooks, did, however, give me somewhere new to go with all of it – not that I started writing overnight, just now and again, until my scribbles started turning themselves into words.

Anyway, the morning in question must have been three or so days after the redhead's first visit, and I'd already forgotten about her. It doesn't take long for the days to melt into each other again like hot slabs of soft metal. What appeared to be my suicide attempt, and the commotion that followed, was by far the most exciting thing to have happened to me in months, if not years. Yet, even that already seemed far off, like something I had read down in the hospital library.

On that morning, something out of the ordinary happened. As I sat making a rough sketch of the path and the fence, and the rocky ridge beyond it, a motorcade of three large, black vehicles crossed the ridge and slowly made their way down toward us.

All three came to a standstill in the parking lot outside the main gate – for security reasons there was parking both inside and outside the grounds of the facility. The three cars stood lined up side by side facing straight toward us, as if they were waiting for it to get dark so that they could light up the place with their headlights. It was the middle of the day, though, and Jonathan had mentioned earlier that he'd wager it would reach 40 degrees out in the sun.

A small black man in a suit got out and marched toward the guardhouse at the gate. He and the guard talked for a minute and then the visitor turned and beckoned towards his companions. People poured out of the three cars, about ten all in all – the men wearing dark suits, the two women dressed in heavy, colourful robes that seemed to weigh them down in the heat.

They stood around aimlessly, occasionally looking up at the building and gesturing, talking among themselves. Then I saw Von Hansmeyer walking briskly down the driveway. The guard opened the gate and let the doctor out, pulling it closed again behind him.

Von Hansmeyer walked straight to a plump, bespectacled man who held out a hand for him to shake. They talked for a few minutes, Von Hansmeyer gesticulating toward the hospital. And then, quite suddenly, the visitors climbed back into their cars and drove back up the hill, out of sight, back to the outside world.

For a moment Von Hansmeyer stood looking after them – a white coat alone out there under the beating sun. He turned around slowly and, absent-mindedly, made his way back to his flock of coughing corpses. I almost felt sorry for him.

'You know who that was, Barry?' Jonathan said behind me, startling me so that my pencil went clattering to the floor. He bent to pick it up. 'That was the premier of the Eastern Cape. He came to have a look at the freak show.'

'He couldn't have seen much,' I said.

'No, sirree, but he can tell his fat-cat buddies that he's been here and seen what things are like. We'll probably read about it in tomorrow's paper.'

Jonathan handed me the pencil and stood hands on hips, looking out at the ridge, where the remnants of dust cloud were still visible. His body was lanky and muscular next to me. A warm smell of detergent hung about him.

He coughed violently. It was tinny, as if his insides were constructed out of a rusty clockwork of springs and thin metal sheets. It sounded so unnatural that I wondered if he was about to disintegrate into a pile of iron filings, his voice morphing into indecipherable static.

I was relieved when he straightened up and cleared his throat, coughing up a wad of milky phlegm into the snow-white handkerchief retrieved from his trouser pocket. Even though I had shared a ward with him for more than a year, I felt I hardly knew him. I certainly hadn't contemplated him dying on me.

'You all right? I asked.

'Yes, sport. Just swallowed a fly.'

Story goes Jonathan had been a mechanic in Cape Town when the bug caught up with him. They say he figured it out before they could lock him up, so he sold up what he could and decided to it the road, take a holiday. Eventually, though, you get too sick, and if they don't pick your corpse out of some ditch next to the highway, you end up here.

They say a neighbour found him half dead in a beach house some place on the west coast, but I had never felt like asking him about it. Some part of me likes the idea of him hiding out in a desolate little wind-swept cottage in some nameless town, whisky bottles lined up next to the bed, and a stack of dirty magazines for company.

But that's just me daydreaming.

No one really knows how Jonathan found his way into the hospital.

He doesn't talk about lost kids, dogs, women, or long-forgotten jobs like most of the others. Or maybe he used to, and just got tired of repeating himself.

'The bastard is too scared to come in here. Too scared he might catch the bug himself,' he said.

'Can't exactly blame him, can you?'

'Well, he should at least take a closer look if he's going to shut us down or move us out or whatever he's thinking up.

You must know that all this is not forever, Barry.' He spread his arms to indicate the buildings and fences around us. 'Just last week I read in the *Times* that those upstart lefty lawyers in Joburg are planning to take the government to court about the constitutionality of locking us up.'

'No, I don't know,' I said. I wanted to say that it all seemed pretty forever to me, but I decided against it.

'You don't agree, sport?' he said. 'Well, let's just wait and see then, shall we? There's something in the air, that's for sure. The storm is beginning to blow over. The plague is already old news. Something is about to change, I know that much...'

'The premier seemed pretty scared to me,' I said.

'You just wait, sport – just you wait and see.'

Jonathan and I stood looking out at the disappearing dust cloud left by the retreating motorcade of Eastern Cape leadership. No doubt they were already eclipsing the speed limit on their way back to Port Elizabeth, blue lights flashing all the way.

IS THERE REALLY ANY reason to be that scared of us, I wonder. Any reason not to put on a mask and pass through the gate, but instead to gawk at us from a distance? I know we're out of bounds to the world, but are we really that different, *that* infectious? Does a simple bacterial infection really change who or what we are? Or is it being locked up that makes us different? Have we, merely by being here, become something else? Have we been infected with something other than the bacterium?

Another day altogether. Staring out of the ward window, again there is a movement on the horizon, a dust storm gathering. Not a government convoy this time, but a crowded yellow Mazda, which finally pulls up on the far side of the fence. Two women and a kid of about five climb out, possibly three generations of the same family. The woman in her thirties goes over to speak to the guard. Her braids, her bright red T-shirt, her child with white sandals. Not a rich family, but not starving. Two others remain seated in the car, although I see only their darkened silhouettes and can't make them out. Are they the men of the family, or just friends of the women, or people they have paid for the ride?

And then Kagiso, of all people, appears at the front door of the hospital and makes his way over to the fence where they the women and child are waiting. It comes as a shock. Kagiso is probably the hardest man in this place. He was a gangster on the outside and he's a gangster on the inside.

He has had to put on a mask and stands talking to the two women on the other side of the fence. They don't try to touch each other, no hands pressed through the fence, just some words exchanged, the girl suddenly terribly shy, hiding behind what I assume to be her mother and then running back to the car and slamming the door behind her.

This is the same Kagiso who somehow manages to get his hands on cartons of cigarettes and who pays younger men for their urine samples so that he can fake his monthly tests. The same man who always carries a knife and for whom the head of a table in the dining hall is always left open. This is the same Kagiso who just the other day knocked Espoir's dinner tray out of his hands and then squared up to look Espoir in the eyes, daring him to do something about it. Espoir just stood there, the only movement the slight twitch of a muscle in his arm that sent ripples through his snake tattoo.

There is no physical contact between Kagiso and the woman he is talking to, no sign of emotion except maybe for the child running off. Just a few sentences exchanged. He must know, as I do, that the outside world is best forgotten, that that little girl can now only bring him pain.

THE NIGHT BEFORE THE redhead was to come see me again, I woke up with the taste of blood in my throat. I tried to scream, but all that came out was a soft gurgling. I couldn't breathe. So I rolled over. After a protracted fit of deep-throat coughing, I managed to hack out a thick, bloody goo.

It was late, moonlight streamed pale through the window, and for a moment I wondered if I had been dreaming. The soft lunar light in the room felt strangely familiar, like something from a barely remembered childhood nightmare.

I screamed.

Once again, my throat seemed to contract, as if a rope was pulled tight around it. I felt an obscenely large mass of gunk gush out my nose. I think I heard Jonathan mumble something, and then suddenly the lights were on and the broad-shouldered Dugan was trying to look into my eyes while a stout young nurse plunged a needle into my arm.

I can't remember much more of that night. What I lay thinking about when I woke the next morning, well drugged and drowsy, lying under clean sheets in the emergency ward, was how terrified I had been as I had struggled for air. I shuddered as I remembered the feeling of that thick glob building up pressure and then splattering from my nose.

Despite the raw, inflamed nasal membranes and throat, the air felt cool, pure and translucent. I held on to it for a second like one holds on to a joint. That morning it felt as if both my throat and nose had been cleared out and covered with a thin residue of mint-flavoured tile cleaner.

In the many months I had spent in the hospital I thought I had come to terms with the reaper. I had imagined walking up to him, tapping on his plastic mask, and saying something funny that had all the guys laughing in the waiting room up there at the gates of hell.

Yet, as I lay there, my blood doing its best to get out of and away from my body, I felt an indefinable terror. I couldn't really say exactly what I was so terrified of. Maybe it was just instinct. Maybe the disease will leave my instincts intact, will leave itself a little something to offer resistance when the game is almost over.

Von Hansmeyer came to check up on me. He said that I had had a nodular rupture and that it wasn't all that much to be worried about. Peering through his round spectacles, he grinned and said in that German accent of his, 'You were lucky, Barry. It could have been much worse.'

He said that nodules burst sometimes and that there was nothing you could do to stop it.

'It is so messy because you are coughing up all the newly freed blood and pus... When you can't cough it out is when you have a problem.'

He stood staring past me for a moment, and then reminded me that Ms Van Vuuren would be coming to see me.

And indeed, after falling asleep and then waking again more times than I can remember, I saw her sitting next to the bed, her figure smaller than I remembered, just a silhouette outlined on a chair. I felt her more than saw her.

I didn't say anything and drifted off, back into the fever dream about a long-gone school day I had been revisiting all day. One moment I was struggling to keep together the pages of a history essay I had to hand in, the next I was trying to explain to an angry teacher that my school blazer was too small and that it no longer fit me. And then I was looking for a way out of the school hall so that I could get to the construction job I was working in my off period.

When I opened my eyes, Van Vuuren was still there, looking straight at me, a clean white mask drawn tight over her mouth and nose. I lay for a while trying to remember if she had worn a mask when we had talked before. I was sure she hadn't, but why then hadn't that stayed with me, made more of an impression? Except for Von Hansmeyer, everyone wore masks.

'How are you feeling?' she said in a quiet voice that seemed not to come from her, but from somewhere far behind her.

'Drugged,' I said.

'Can I get you anything?'

'No. Just stay a bit.'

When I came to again, she was gone, and all that remained of her was the faintest trace of that lavender-scented perfume. It hung lingering in the air like the rustle of a dress.

I lay listening to the sounds of the hospital. Other than the steady thrum of insects in the stifling heat beyond the window, the emergency ward was unusually quiet. It was summer. We all do better in the summer months, when the Karoo dries out. They say our sick lungs prefer the dry, hot air.

There were eight beds in the ward. Apart from the hairy foot that stuck out from behind a half-drawn green curtain, I was alone.

As I lay there, the everyday echoes of the hospital slowly seeped into the ward and for a long time, I just absorbed the sounds of the place. There was something soothing about the distant coughing, the whoosh of plumbing, footsteps in the corridor, the guards joking in heavily accented Afrikaans. These were things I never noticed.

Whatever they had given me had dulled any discomfort there may have been. I felt a strange calmness come over me, a calmness like that which sometimes settles over me when I'm staring out my ward window. I like toying with the idea that it is a foretaste of death. There is a sense of endlessness about it, as if I've been sitting in some long-dead deity's waiting room for ages, about to be buzzed into nothingness. It didn't feel scary, and I didn't feel trapped. It was just peaceful waiting.

Then I thought of the small, quiet silhouette that had sat next to my bed and how dark this silhouette was, and I couldn't get away from the feeling that it was like a dark flame sitting there burning for me.

Whether in waiting or in judgment, or just for no reason at all, I could not tell.

marginalia

OBSERVATIONS FROM JAMES' NARRATIVE in this initial section of the second notebook make it clear that, despite what transpires in further volumes of his writing, James' relationship with Mr Jonathan Fox is not a close one. By his account here and descriptions later, it is not a comfortable liaison. In fact, James appears to be agitated by Fox, irritated by his mannerisms and affectations. A cursory analysis may reveal that it is perhaps because Fox himself is not only a foil to James's own meanderings of the mind, but also a shadow of himself – one whose origins defy his present reality, a theatre of the mind and body playing itself on a stage of neither's choosing. But, whereas James himself is focused on the interplay between thought and deed, Fox relies purely on the here-and-now, the reality of their existing world.

WAKING UP. MUCH LATER. Still in emergency. My throat and nose weren't feeling quite as raw. My head seemed clearer than it had in a long time. Which is not to say that things didn't still seem too bright and too loud.

'What happened to you, then?' asked Jonathan. 'You left in such a hurry, never even said goodbye.'

'Burst nodules,' I said.

'Those blasted nodules,' he said, pulling up a chair and sitting down. You wouldn't say Jonathan was so sick as to be quarantined if you looked at him. Not then, anyway.

He unfolded a newspaper he had carried under his arm like a sergeant major on parade. Spreading it open, he lifted a page to show me a picture of a man behind a microphone with his arm raised, his face scrunched up with intensity.

'Do you recognise him?'

'Yes, he's the one who came to check us out.'

'Exactly,' Jonathan said, 'The premier himself. And do you know what he's talking about?'

'Well, yes, while they were wheeling me in here I asked them to stop by the library for a cup of tea and a read... No, of course I don't know.'

Jonathan looked at me with mock impatience. 'Well, it

43

says here, "Premier Nkonyeni denied allegations that the province will soon be incapable of paying the wages of health workers", and "he also reasserted the province's dedication to containing the outbreak of pulmonary nodulosis and denied suggestions that economic difficulties would make the continued implementation of the national strategic plan an impossibility in the region."'

He let the paper drop to his lap and looked at me. 'You know what that means?'

'We're getting ice cream for dinner?' I said.

'One word: trouble. Trouble. The fool doesn't have any clue what he's doing. Do you think all our nice nurses would be here if their salaries weren't being paid? And what if the pills dry up? I see the signs, Barry, and let me tell you, they are not looking good. He came here because he was worried. He never gave a damn about us before.'

'I suppose that could be. Maybe he was just curious, though?'

'Yes, Barry,' he said and sighed. 'Either way, if what this newspaper report suggests is true, the province is running out of money, just like the rest of the country.'

He picked up the paper again. 'Look here,' he said. 'They say Volkswagen is going to close down all operations in the Eastern Cape. "In five years' time it is expected that employment in the vehicle-manufacturing industry in the Eastern Cape will drop to zero." No cars being made or put together in the Eastern Cape whatsoever. That is unheard of, I tell you. Unheard of.'

'What about the uranium?'

'What about it? The mines outside Beaufort have all been abandoned.'

'I didn't know that.'

'Happened months ago. Some dispute over ownership. It is all corrupt, sport, corrupt to the bloody core.'

'I hear you,' I managed, but my attention was slipping.

In a space far behind my eyes I felt a headache coming on,

a freight train threatening to sweep me up and carry me off, back into sleep. Or, if they didn't give me more of those fine opiates in time, it would just crash mercilessly into my skull.

I moaned.

'Should I get a nurse, sport?' Jonathan asked, rolled-up paper in his hand.

Before the nurse could get to me, the train crashed, my senses blurring into slow motion as something ruptured and I blacked out.

Two days later von hansmeyer said I could return to my ward. That was the thing with nodules: out of the blue they almost killed you and then just as suddenly the threat was over. It took a few weeks for your lungs to deal with all the scarring, but if you survived the first night, you'd be okay.

I spent most of the following days in bed. I slept more than I had in years. Whatever meds they had me on put me out like a horse. Twice every day a nurse would tap his foot while I trudged up and down the corridor to exercise my lungs. It was slow going.

One afternoon, from my bed in my ward, I heard shouting. A door slammed. Something clattered to the ground. I was too tired to get up to look, but later that day Jonathan hurried up to the room to tell me that the gangs had had a bust-up.

'Something happened in the showers,' he said, strangely excited by it all. 'There is a lot of blood.' He didn't know more. I didn't really care much either. I was feeling too rotten. I didn't give it another thought.

Then, late one afternoon, probably a week or so into my recovery, as I was slowly making my way back from my daily exercise routine up and down the corridor, I saw Kagiso and Sibu heading in the direction of the stairs. They looked like they meant business. I think it was something about the narrow-eyed, determined expression on Kagiso's face that made me stop and then follow them at a distance. I noticed his hand on a long narrow object in his pocket and remembered that he had a knife. I heard Kagiso say, 'I'm going to pulp the fucking kwere's head.' I remembered the afternoon of the distant shouting and the blood in the bathroom.

My legs felt weak. I had to lean against the wall as I walked. My head pounded a rhythm that made me feel faint on each beat. The hospital swivelled around me. I thought of just letting them be, but remembering Jonathan's story of the blood in the showers, I pushed on after them. Like everyone else, I was starved of excitement.

From the landing, I saw through the large window that lit up the stairs that they were already out in the back yard. They loped over to where Espoir and his gang of African refugees were sitting with their legs stretched out on the concrete, their backs against the wall of the laundry room. I knew that that wall would be baked hot from the day's sun, offering a certain comforting warmth that time of evening. If I hadn't been feeling so awful I might have gone down myself.

Espoir didn't get up when Kagiso came to a standstill in front of them. As he sat there, his long limbs shiny, perfectly shaped, he looked so bored and disinterested that I wondered where he was stoned or in some suninduced delirium.

Kagiso said something, but Espoir simply ignored him. Then Kagiso started shouting and waving his arms about at the jaded man on the ground. It looked as if he was about to kick him, but Sibu held him back.

A crowd of patients gathered around as if they had been waiting for this confrontation for years. They started a slow clap.

Kagiso turned and spoke, addressing the bystanders as much as the men on the ground. He made a sweeping gesture with his arms. He looked up at the empty sky. Then, suddenly, he spun around. He bent down toward Espoir and hissed something, saliva spraying as he did so.

From where I was standing it all seemed to happen in silent-movie slow motion. No sound breached the window. All I could hear was the distant clatter of plates being washed in the kitchen. It sounded like any other afternoon in the hospital.

As I reached up to open the upper window a crack to let the outside in, Espoir's arm shot out. In one fluid motion, he reached out amd managed to grab Kagiso by the ear, yanking him head first down into the concrete. The bystanders roared and whistled. The impact couldn't have been very hard though, because a moment later Kagiso was back up, trying to knee Espoir in the face. He connected with his chest instead, and Espoir staggered sideways. He struggled to get up on his feet, and before he could find his balance, Kagiso launched himself at the Senegalese man. They both dropped to the ground like lame horses.

A blur of rummaging limbs, legs kicking wildly, fists flying, arms flailing about. Two heaving, grunting beasts wrestling on the hard concrete, their sweaty bodies thrashing around in the fine red dust, hands seeking a grip. Then a smear of crimson on the grey concrete. A head slammed down into the ground, a chilling crack met with a sudden stunned silence. Dead silence. No cheer from the onlookers. No clapping.

As I stood there, watching from the relative quiet of the landing, it all looked wrong. I had seen a fight or two in my life, and this wasn't one. Then, as Kagiso let go of Espoir's neck and it slumped to the concrete, I caught a momentary glimpse of Kagiso's face, not enraged, but dead and sickly looking. These were not men fighting, but corpses.

I looked away. A deep nausea welled up in my throat. What the fuck had we come to? If I hadn't been sick just a few minutes ago, I might have been then.

Quite suddenly, it was all over. The brawl had lasted only a matter of seconds. Now, except for two heaving chests, the tangle of limbs and torsos lay unmoving. Their mingling blood pooling a reddish brown. After a while, Kagiso struggled up slowly and started dusting himself off amidst a heavy fit of coughing. On the ground, Espoir lay curled up, convulsing, coughing lumps of bloody gunk. On the ground near his feet a bright object, maybe a knife, flashed in the failing light.

The bystanders stood, not knowing where to look. Some turned and slumped away. From the door below I saw the clean white of a nurse's uniform running out to Espoir. He was still coughing blood. Kagiso and Sibu were nowhere to be seen. The nurse turned back and shouted urgently for help, and soon afterwards a second nurse and then Von Hansmeyer went rushing out, the doctor's balding head gleaming in the late afternoon.

I turned around and trudged back up to my ward. I shouldn't have followed them.

Later that evening an ambulance came for Espoir. We never saw him again. The story was that he had been badly cut and had to be treated at the big state hospital in Port Elizabeth. Maybe he got better and just wasn't sent back to us, maybe he bled to death; no one knows.

Kagiso stayed in emergency a full three days, not for the knife wound in his side, but to stabilise his airways. The problem wasn't any injury, but that the bug had been reawakened inside him and was taking its revenge on his lungs and oesophagus.

That was the last fight I saw. There were more – of course there were – but something changed. We had lost the capacity for such things, stopped seeking them out, chasing after them, cheering from the sidelines, not because our minds were purified, but because our bodies were sick. We just weren't men any more, not in the way we used to be. Some people were in denial about this, of course, but most people knew.

Sarah would have laughed had she heard me saying that. She would have said that's nonsense and that being a man has nothing to do with fighting. But she would have been wrong.

And even if she'd seen that sad struggle out in the yard, I'm not sure she would have been able to grasp what it meant. Every patient who saw it knew exactly what it meant. It knocked the bottom out of your capacity to want anything, if that hadn't been knocked out a long time ago.

THE NEXT TIME I got to the dusty room next to Von Hansmeyer's office, she was already sitting behind the desk waiting, the door ajar. She looked up at me and from her eyes I guessed she was smiling behind the mask.

I closed the door behind me and sat down. A spicy fragrance, not the lavender from before, hung in the air, as if she had brought with her a ghost one could only smell. I sat inhaling it for a moment.

'How are you, Barry? Feeling any better?'

I noticed something tender about her, her eyes, that I hadn't noticed before. Something seemed to have changed – in me rather than her. It was as if the ruptured nodules had flushed away some reservoir of resistance. I knew that making any kind of connection with someone from the outside would be dangerous, especially a young woman like her. Still, I felt myself going with it.

'Yes, much better. Not at all bad for someone on death row.'

'I visited you when you were in the emergency room last week,' she said after a long silence. She looked straight at me, a look that seemed to say she was proud of herself for having made the sacrifice. 'Did you know I was there?'

'I noticed.'

'You asked me to stay,' she said softly.

'I did?'

'Yes, you did.'

'Well, you weren't there when I woke up.'

'Well, Barry!' she laughed. 'You were out for a very long time. I couldn't wait forever. Besides, I don't like driving back to town in the dark. I did wait for a long time. You really shouldn't feel let down.'

'Thank you then.' I thought of her silhouette again, next to my bed like a dark flame, burning with that hypnotic intensity. I even thought of telling her about the flame, but didn't.

'You do that with all your patients?'

'I visit some people, but not everyone,' she said, her voice trailing off.

We sat in silence for a minute. She didn't seem to mind.

'We didn't get off to a great start, Barry. I'm sorry. I pushed too hard in our first session. It wasn't very professional of me,' she said. 'Can we start again? I promise only to talk about the things you're comfortable discussing.'

I nodded, even though I wasn't sure what we would talk about. What she didn't know was what I was most afraid of was the talking itself. I couldn't let myself be chained to the world again. I couldn't make room for her in my mind and start allowing in the whole business of life on the outside to seep in. That was all over for me.

And yet, when she asked whether I felt like telling her about my life before quarantine, for some reason I said, 'Okay.' I wasn't up to digging up corpses I had buried long ago, but somehow I let myself be drawn out.

There was a long, protracted shout from outside, from in the yard below. She stood up quickly and walked over to the window and stood looking. 'Sorry, its nothing,' she said, almost to herself. 'There's a nurse down there anyway. Where were we?'

But, unbeknown to her, we were no longer anywhere near

where we were. As she had stood there at the window, turned away from me, left to my own devices for a few seconds – and this is the cold heart of it – sitting there in that quiet room, something inside me asked why not other corpses, why not imaginary corpses? And just like that everything was different. Looking back now I can see this flipping of the switch inside me with absolute clarity. Not a decision. Not a scheme. Just a sudden but definitive change of current.

'Err... I'm not sure where to start.' I looked out the window behind her. In my mind's eye I saw dusty graves on a rainy day, a pallid mourner dressed in black. I let the current take me. Let the images come... thick green lawns, horses, expensive cutlery.

'Maybe you can start by telling me about Sarah. She's listed as your next of kin on our files. Is she your mother, your sister? For some reason, it doesn't say.'

The mention of Sarah threw me for a moment. It made no sense. I certainly hadn't given them her name. But then I thought of the graves my mind had conjured, felt the current pulling me, realigning itself around a kink in the river. Yes, why not Sarah? In fact, this was the ideal opening.

'Hell, no,' I said. 'Sarah wasn't family.'

'Why do you say *wasn't*?' she asked.

'I say wasn't, because she's dead.'

'I'm sorry to hear that,' she said, a tentative note in her voice.

I just shrugged.

'Was she your girlfriend?' she asked.

'Yes,' I said, hardly blinking.

There was silence for a moment, before I felt obliged to continue.

'I remember one evening we were out with her family. at some restaurant on a wine farm, all dark wood and white linen, a beautiful place out in Constantia. I'd gone outside for a smoke after dinner. Next thing her father was standing next to me. He was very tall. He didn't look Jewish, but Sarah had told me how his parents had emigrated from Poland in the late thirties. Standing there, watching the sprinklers spinning on the dusky lawns, he asked me about my parents and what my plans were for the future. And then he told me how his parents had struggled to make a life here in Africa and how he too had had to work for everything he had.'

'So he didn't like you?' The psychologist in her was being cautious. Could it be that she doubted me even then?

'Fathers never like me, but this guy was the worst. I could tell he was judging me. That I wasn't good enough for his little girl. Not Rondebosch enough.'

'And the rest of her family? Did you get along better with them?'

'Yes, well, I met her because of her brother. We worked at the same company. Me in security, he in finance. A real mamma's boy. He gave me a lift sometimes in his old Merc. One day he asked me back to his house, which was really his parents' house. That's where I met her. She made it worthwhile being friends with the mama's boy.'

I had no idea where all this was coming from, nor where the current would take me. But I knew it meant nothing. It couldn't tie me down, so I went with it.

Besides, as I later realised, I liked being there with her in that little room. Having to say a few words was a reasonable price to pay for spending an hour a week in a room with a pretty girl with red hair and black stockings. I wasn't going to get carried away, though. Just sitting there with her, listening to the quiet rise and fall of her voice, watching the graceful posture of her back, or catching a glimpse of a shoe with a heel, had the feeling of looking at something both familiar and yet strange and unknown, something I had forgotten existed.

That night I dreamt that it was snowing outside, and even though I recognised the landscape, and I was in my ward, my dream-self knew I was somewhere in Eastern Europe. I was wearing a navy-blue suit I had last worn to church as a teenager. I remember worrying that it looked peculiar on me.

I was standing at the door of the hospital, which was now something of a stately rural retreat, looking out at the cold. From deep inside the building I heard the waxy warmth of violins and the soft murmur of voices. Out front, dark wooden carriages stood parked in a circle. I remember there being something striking about a large black horse that stood perfectly still while snowflakes gently drifted onto its face. He didn't even shake his head or anything, but just stood there.

A man with a deep scar across his cheek stepped out of one of the carriages and said something to me in what I took to be Russian or Polish. I just smiled and the man smiled back, tapped me on the shoulder and indicated that I should join him inside.

In a large ballroom men in tailored suits were dancing with women in white dresses and white gloves that reached above their elbows. Thick, red velvet curtains hung draped from a high ceiling and golden pillars engraved with intricate plant motifs were evenly spaced around the room. On a balcony at the far end of the hall a short, bald man was conducting a small ensemble of violin and cello.

Then, amid the throng of Eastern European gentry, I caught sight of Ms Van Vuuren dancing with Dugan, the large broad-shouldered nurse who handed out the meds. She was wearing her hair up and pulled back tight. I remember thinking that this brought out something young and lively in her. I watched them dance for a while, her graceful with her elegant posture and small shoulders, and him clumsy and disinterested as always.

As I was standing there, an unfathomable jealousy welling up in me, a tall girl with curly blonde hair suddenly grabbed me from behind and led me onto the over-crowded dance floor, waltzing with the rise and fall of a ship at sea – which is exactly how I felt. She kept shouting things to me in German, leaning in with a stale beer breath, always smiling, perspiring profusely on her broad forehead. Even though my legs refused to move, she nevertheless dragged me along. I wanted to apologise, to excuse myself, but I couldn't get a word in.

From time to time, amid all the swinging and twirling and rising and falling, I'd catch a momentary glimpse of Ms Van Vuuren with the broad-shouldered nurse. Each time they seemed to be looking deeper into each other's eyes, and each time he seemed less disinterested. Then I'd be swept away again on the music, doing my best to stay upright.

On the balcony the conductor was swinging his arms about like a man who had lost his mind. Then I saw his baton spinning through the air only to be caught by a large, bearded man who held it up to the light and snapped it in two.

Rather than fading, the music picked up pace, the conductor madly flinging his arms about, faster and faster. And then, somewhere in the turmoil, as it was all coming to an end, I saw the broad frame of the nurse leading Ms Van Vuuren into a little enclave between pillar and curtain and pulling her close, and her yielding her neatly painted lips to him.

Just then, as the German girl came to a standstill and I felt the sweat-drenched fabric in the small of her back, I felt a shudder of disgust. And I woke.

DAYS DRAG LIKE DRAG nets
like a police search for a body
out on the windy waste
out where a corpse lies waiting
in here we are the reborn dead
in here they'll never find us
never mind the line of quiet uniforms
searching, their eyes to the ground
they'll walk right by us
we have fallen from their world
they should change our names when they lock us up
call us by otherworldly numbers
cut the cord that holds us here
and set us free

marginalia

ONE OF THE MOST striking stylistic aspects of Mr James' journals is the way in which the text vacillates between vivid, descriptive narrative and stark, terse writing. Although he writes mostly with a relatively clear and distinct voice, there are indications that he is experimenting with both style and content. Whereas notebooks* Three and Four are notable in their staccatolike note form, books Five Through Seven*, for instance, are liberally scattered with modifying adjectives and adverbial phrases that lend the writing an almost poetic quality, to suggest that despite his initial reluctance and reservations, he gradually took to the notion of expressing himself in words, in ink on paper, developing a style of expression more visceral in content than seen in the other volumes. Of course, it cannot be discounted that these variations are in fact intentional, that Mr James remained throughout this period conscious of readers and critics.

This poem is an example of such experimentation in form. James did not self-identify as a poet and appeared not to have written much poetry – there are only two completed poems in the journals. Analysis of ink-patterns in the water-damaged sections of the first notebook suggest that it may have contained more poems, but at this stage it remains conjecture.

A T NIGHT JONATHAN OFTEN makes a strange wheezing sound as he sleeps. It is not loud, or anything like the snoring one hears in any of the other wards. It is a quiet inhuman whirr, as if there is some tiny, malfunctioning mechanism lodged in his throat.

When we're shooting pool in the rec room, the sleeping man with the thing in his throat is unimaginable. He is in harmony with everything around him, his eyes darting around, acknowledging passers-by with little nods and winks, his graceful hand on the scuffed green of the pool table, head tilting when he looks at you – never letting on that he is always calculating. Known by everyone, if not necessarily liked. If anyone is our leader, he is. Our poor-man's Mr Kurtz.

Most of the time you wouldn't say he was sick. Sure, his cheeks were sunken and he certainly had nights when he kept me awake with his coughing, but he never looked like someone who was going to die. He seemed content with growing old in the hospital, as if there was nowhere else he'd rather be. After all, he hadn't been party to the first disastrous attempt at escape some months earlier. He actually liked being here, ruling over us all, being our man on the hospital committee.

That is what I used to think.

Then one day things changed. I was sitting as I often do, staring out to where the road meets the ridge, when he came up behind me and leaned in with a hushed voice.

'We might have a way out, Barry, my boy,' he said, as calm as if he was commenting on the weather.

It took me a moment to register what he had said.

'Okay, I guess we might,' I said, but I was just talking. My mind hadn't caught up yet.

'The time is not right yet, but it will be soon,' he said. 'Either way, I think you had better come along. It will do you good to get out of here.' He rested his hand on my shoulder and kept it there.

'Okay,' I said.

Looking back now, the strange thing about that day was that I didn't get excited. I wasn't just playing it cool, trying to stay deadpan while my insides heaved and pulsed. I just didn't feel anything. I had spent all my excitement and pretending in my previous life. In here, even the promise of escape seemed a little dull. And yet I went along with it.

Jonathan had no idea how little I cared about escaping. He probably saw me sitting there, staring out day after day, and imagined that I was obsessing about the outside world. He didn't know that I wasn't thinking about the outside at all, that that stretch of hard Karoo earth was, in fact, the world for me. Whatever lay beyond it no longer existed. I made the mistake of thinking that Jonathan felt the same, that his life was here, and here only. But I was wrong. He wanted out.

Still, when I lay in bed that night I imagined crossing the ridge, seeing the road in front of me and holding out a thumb for one of those large trucks you could hear groaning in the distance when it had been raining.

'Escape.' I rolled the word over my tongue. 'Escape', that word so lightly used on the outside, so sacred in here, the word that meant the road and the city and long-legged girls in stockings and cool rolling lawns and windy beaches and the deep blue ocean. The word that was everything but this slow, slow dying.

And, of course, Jonathan being Jonathan never let it go. The next day he pulled me aside after lunch. We went for a walk in the courtyard at the back of the hospital. We were always being encouraged to go for walks. The dry air and exercise were good for us apparently. Either way, it was the only way to get a little of anything that resembled privacy.

We walked along the tall electrified perimeter of the back fence. Beyond it the semi-desert of the Karoo lay dead, hard and flat. I stood looking out over it and for the first time in years I felt like a cigarette.

Jonathan stopped. We stood for a minute looking out into the distance. There were no clouds, no mountains, no buildings, just the flat, dried-up bottom of an unimaginably large lake.

'I went to the management committee meeting yesterday,' said Jonathan, our elected representative when it came to all things official and bureaucratic. 'It seems they might have to lay some people off. The staff are very tense. It's a good time for us, Barry. A good time.'

'You mean they won't care if we sneak out? They'll look the other way?'

He snorted in a feeble attempt at a laugh. 'Something like that, sport. Some cracks might start to appear in hospital security, that's all I'm saying. Besides, we already have one of the guards in a tight spot and willing to cooperate. If we're lucky, that will be enough.'

'Well done. So, are we digging a tunnel?'

He kicked at the ground at our feet as if to test its firmness. A small plume of dust sprung up and then was gone again. He looked at it intently. 'Well, there are a number of options. We haven't figured it all out yet. But we're thinking that we'll have to sabotage the floodlights and kill the current in the fence. We might have to dig. Maybe, if everything works out, we could just cut our way through. It'll be tricky, but it might just work out.'

We were walking again now. From far above us the sun beat down its shards of nuclear radiation. I felt a bead of sweat running down my neck. 'Who's this "we" you keep talking about?'

'Does it matter?'

'I don't suppose it does really,' I shrugged.

'Hell, you can be such a pushover sometimes, Barry. It's quite predictable really. While you were sleeping off your burst nodules, Kagiso came to see me. He says they have something on one of the guards. I didn't ask too many questions. You know what Kagiso is like. He wants me to help figure out the best way to do it. He's convinced we'll have only one shot at it. For some reason, he also thought I'd know something about switching off the current in the fence.'

'Who is the inside man then?'

'They're not telling me. But they'll have to sooner or later.'

'I'm not sure about Kagiso,' I said. 'I don't trust him.'

'Jesus, Barry! Is that all you can do? Stand there and find fault.' There was a sharp, girlish harshness to his tone now. 'This is your fucking chance to get out of this hellhole. You just want to sit here and die? Dammit, man! I'm not asking the whole hospital to come along. I'm asking you. Don't be so damn ungrateful.'

I waited for him to calm down. We had come to the corner of the back yard. Far over the horizon to the east I thought I saw a thin column of smoke rising. It was hard to tell if it was real.

'I'm not exactly ungrateful,' I said, but as I said it I knew the way that I had said it was all wrong.

'Fuck it, man!' he spat and moved off, leaving me alone out there. He stalked across the yard to the large doors that opened out of the main corridor on the lower level. His steps were long and quick like those of a man who knew exactly where he was going.

There was something odd about the way his head was tilted slightly to the left. I had never noticed that before. I wondered if that had anything to do with the bug. Maybe the infection had spread up his spine. Or maybe it was an injury from before, something that happened in a workshop in Goodwood or some other semi-industrial suburb from his other life, his life before here.

I turned and looked back out over the waste beyond the fence. Then I looked at the fence itself. The hard galvanised pole in front of me had an opaque sheen to it. It may have been just a piece of metal, but it meant that men like Jonathan and Kagiso had to devise plans for their freedom, that grown men had to have secret meetings in the back yards of quarantine hospitals.

Then I thought about how different a pole looked from up close. I had gotten used to staring at the poles at the front of the building from my seat at our ward window, but seeing a pole like this was different. It wasn't part of a bigger picture, just a stupid, inanimate everyday object. Simply standing there. Still, I stood there for a while and considered marking it as my own.

And then I did.

OUTSIDE THE WARD WINDOW, the Karoo is a deathly dull grey. Looking at it is like staring through a hole in the fabric of reality. You don't see anything beyond it, though, just more of the same old nothingness.

I guess I'm not feeling good. But that's okay. Happens to all of us, it seems. It's just that it's happening more and more. I used to think it was the pills that did it, that took the last of the life that I had in me and dissolved it, made me breathe it out without even noticing. Blaming the meds is bullshit though.

Every day I just sit here. And every day just rolls over into another. I don't talk to anyone any more, and I see much the same in some of the others. Sure, we're all dying, there's no denying it. But that's not it. Here where we are, we've seen what we shouldn't have.

Then again, maybe it's just me; maybe I went hollow inside when Sarah died. I used to think that. But I don't know. Not for sure, anyway. Maybe I was always hollow inside.

All that sounds a little melodramatic, I know, but what do you do when you sit in front of a window day after day staring at a dead stretch of earth with a fence around it, all the time listening to people around you cough their way to death?

'We'll tar the roads to hell with the tar in our lungs. And

what heavenly choir of prostitutes, pimps and degenerates there awaits us we greet with salutations of despair.'

As I write these lines Jonathan is lying on his bed, his breathing deep and regular. He had been complaining earlier that he felt like a burnt-out chassis after a car wreck. He had a pale, washed-out look about him and, for the first time since I've known him, one could tell that he had the bug. I didn't say anything, though. Ever since the encounter in the yard we hadn't been talking.

I don't suppose I can blame him.

Still, whatever hope Jonathan imagines out there is utter bullshit.

He knows it too, I'm sure. Deep down, we all know it. There's nothing beyond that fence but a ghastly, throw-away wasteland. He needs to move, that's all. Maybe he knows it's pointless and it is the moving itself that makes him want to do this, attempt this dramatic escape, be a fucking hero.

And even though I'm here with him, I can't make the move. I just don't have it in me. I cannot get excited about escaping to a place that no longer exists.

There is no way for me to explain this to him. Besides, I wouldn't expect him – or even want him – to understand. Let him have his dream if that's what it is that's giving him something to live for. I wouldn't want to take that away. Let him be angry at me. It doesn't matter. I'm not going to fake excitement. I've come too far.

I DREAMT THERE WAS a queer white light in the ward. A strange, toxic mist had drifted in through an open window. It smelt like wet cement. I walked over to the window to close it.

Beyond the ridge I saw the smoke of a massive fire just beyond the horizon. It billowed up into the sky in thick black plumes. Where the gates were supposed to be along the fence below the window, there was nothing. The parking lot was empty except for a dead tree that lay across three or four bays in the far corner.

Inside, the ward was empty. Jonathan's bed was neatly made. There was a deathly quiet. I stepped into the corridor, stopped and listened. Still nothing. I walked over to Von Hansmeyer's office. The door stood open. I looked in, but he wasn't there. His glasses lay on his desk, some books scattered on the floor. His phone was off the hook.

Nothing of all this surprised me. As my dream self stood in Von Hansmeyer's office, I wondered whether this breakdown, this complete destruction, wasn't the inevitable end of a place like this, especially at a time like this. Aren't all governments temporary, all societies in flux, all hospitals nothing but sandbags to stop the inevitable flood of death?

Yet, even though everything was wrong, it was also exactly as it should be.

Still in my dream state, I made my way back along the corridor and down the stairs. Alongside the door to the dining hall I found an upturned cart, medical supplies scattered over the floor. Still no one. I pressed open the cold steel door of the room where they kept the stiffs. I don't know what I was hoping to find. Maybe Von Hansmeyer's outstretched body, his eyes milky, swollen balls, the red glow finally subsiding from his cheeks.

But he wasn't there. There was no one there. I stood in the doorway listening to the silence. Already a fine layer of dust and soot from the distant fire was settling over everything. I could hear the ash falling.

Then I thought I heard a creak, as if someone was pushing open a gate that had long been rusted shut. My pulse began to race. I turned around and started looking in all the downstairs wards, the offices, the kitchen. Even though there was no one, I couldn't shake the feeling that there was something strange nearby, lurking beyond some unseen corner.

I pushed open the front door. It was extremely bright outside, colours washed out in the scorching heat of both sun and fire. I crossed the parking lot to where the gates should have been and stood, waiting for the exhilaration of imminent freedom. But it wouldn't come.

Ahead of me was the ridge. Beyond it the smoke was still dark and grey against the sky. I began to make my way down the driveway toward the ridge, where the smoke was darkest, at its most dense. From the top of the ridge I saw the road some hundred metres off. There weren't any cars.

In the far distance I heard a strange whirring sound that sent chills through my whole body. I needed to hide. I crouched down in a deep, scruffy ditch eroded from the dry, hard earth. The sound was coming closer. And then I saw it. It was a car like any other, except it had a loose-fitting, blue plastic wrapping round its wheels. It was the flapping of these bags that was making the unnerving noise that terrified me. The car moved slowly, as if its occupant was on the lookout for something. I imagined eyes darting back and forth scanning the open veld.

I could make out no more than an elongated shape behind the steering wheel, but I knew that whatever was in the car was the uneasy presence I had felt back in the hospital. And still the flapping of those light blue wheel bags came closer. It haunted me, terrified me more than anything I can ever remember.

'They held within their unearthly whirr the essence of some entity so foreign from our world as to make all earthly horror seem but the playthings of children.'

When I woke, I was drenched in a cold, sticky sweat. I rolled onto my side and peered out of the window. Judging by the light, it must have been about four or five. Above the horizon, the sky was already being stained with a milky coldness.

I had been shaken by the dream. Something about that sound still echoed within my mind, the terror as fresh as if I was still huddled out there across the ridge. But I wasn't. So I pulled the sheet tight about me and told myself that it was all over.

But I was wide awake now. So I lay on my side, trying to catch the sky in the moment of changing. The day was slow in coming.

As I lay there, sheet up to my chin, as if from nowhere I remembered a fishing trip once long ago, I remembered the coldness of the air on my face and hands, the quiet of the water with the mist rising from it.

I had gone with an uncle or someone – it wasn't my dad. We had struggled through some thick undergrowth to get to the small dam that lay cool and pale in the predawn sanctity. I remembered the feeling of papery thorns sucking through my socks and scratching my ankles.

It must have been the first and only fish I ever caught.

Of the catching I remember nothing. I just remember the glittering scales as it lay on some shale, one round eye looking straight up at the sky, only the faintest of quivers in the tea-brown, hard jelly of his eyeball. Then suddenly it slapped its tail and leapt a centimetre or two off the ground.

And then I had to bash its head against a stone to put it out of its misery.

I lay for some time trying to remember where this dam was and whom I had gone with, but I couldn't. Still, the memory of that fish and what it felt like to sit next to that dam was as clear as though it had all been just a day or two ago.

Then I remembered my mother waking me up early one morning during the school holidays, and sleeping in the backseat as we drove through the cold, dark morning to some distant family member, now also long forgotten. I tried to shake off the memories. There was no place for them here.

I started coughing. My lungs suddenly felt heavy. I turned onto my back to let the pus-filled weights inside me rest more easily. They felt enormous, as if the organs that were once my lungs were on the verge of crushing everything else in my chest. I lay still and tried to breathe as best as I could: short, shallow breaths. But with each inhale I felt the sickening sludge shift and grow, preparing to spread whatever inflammation it could, all to paralyse its sad host. I felt it draining the strength from my limbs, and wondered if I'd even manage to stand once it was light outside.

I WAITED FOR HER in the same chair in the same room as before. I got up to open the window. Down below two patients were sitting on a low wall, neither saying a word to each other. They sat like that for at least two minutes, hardly even moving to shift their weight. One had a crop of short, curly hair with a scar running down his left temple. I found it strange that I had not noticed him before. The other seemed familiar, but thinking back now I can't place him either.

A bank of low, grey cloud hung far above the two of them like a blue sky in a black-and-white movie. I breathed the air as deep into my scarred lungs as I could. Outside it was hot and stuffy with the promise of rain lingering just out of reach. The bank of cloud was building up, and sooner or later it would erupt. Or maybe it wouldn't. Maybe we would be passed by and the clouds would drop their bounty 500 kilometres further the east, where they hardly needed it.

Leaving the windows wide open, I turned back to my chair and sat down. A gentle breeze, now warm, now cool, rustled through the room. It seemed indecisive, as if nature itself didn't care enough to make up its mind.

Footsteps in the hall. A moment later she entered, her dark lipstick smeared, a strand of hair hanging down her face.

'Sorry I'm late, Barry,' she said, out of breath. 'I just couldn't get away.'

She shrugged off a thick, dark grey jacket and sat down behind the desk. Then, as if suddenly realising that the window behind her was open, she turned in her chair and sat like that for a moment, looking out to where there now seemed to be something darker about the clouds. As she looked out, a single ray of sunlight broke through the gloom.

Then she looked back at me.

'So how are you, Barry?'

But before I could answer, she gave a little yelp and reached for her bag, laughing. From it she took a crumpled mask she had obviously used before and slid it over her head. That must have been the day I saw her lips.

'I'm okay,' I said. 'But maybe I should be asking you the same question?' The little I could still see of her cheeks turned red.

She bent down and pulled two books from her bag.

'I brought you these,' she said, and handed them to me over the desk.

As I reached for them, I caught a whiff of a spicy dark perfume that took me back to a rainy day in Cape Town many years ago.

'*The Black Dahlia*,' I read aloud. 'And *Out of Sight*. Thank you.' I had mentioned to her in our previous meeting that we were running out of good crime novels in the library.

'You seem excited today,' I said.

'Well, maybe,' she said. 'But you know we're not here to talk about me.'

'We're both just people,' I said.

After a momentary pause, she nodded, 'Okay, I'll tell you a little more about me some other time. Maybe. Let's just stick to you for now. How are you feeling? How are your lungs?'

'My lungs are as foul as ever,' I said.

And then, for no reason I could think of, I started telling her about the dream I'd had in which the hospital was deserted and I had crossed the ridge. I wasn't sure if I should tell her about the cars with their strange blue wheel covers and the haunting sound they made, but I did. And as I was telling her, I suddenly realised where the image had come from.

Years before, I had worked on a construction site out in Parow. I was doing the clean-up job after the painters and carpenters had done their thing. Thing was, there were these blue plastic covers we had to pull on over our shoes before we could walk around the newly built apartments to make sure we don't drag dirt from the soles of our shoes through the place. Even though the plastic covers in the dream fitted the whole wheel, they were the same, made of the same material, held in place by the same weak elastic.

She listened intently to my dream. And even though I could sense her shrink's mind starting to tick over, I didn't care. I let her analyse me. Why not? What would it matter anyway?

When I was done, she asked whether that god-awful sound reminded me of anything in particulary, and why I thought it had terrified me so much. I told her that I had no idea, but that it had something otherworldly about it.

'Do you think, Barry, that what you feared in your dream might have been death?' she asked.

'You mean that my mind created all that strangeness just because I don't want to face that I might die any day?'

'Something like that. I'm just asking if that makes any sense, seems right to you,' she said, her voice still raspy with the exhilaration of whatever had preceded our meeting.

'I don't know. Probably not,' I said. 'I don't really have any trouble thinking about death.' I was suddenly annoyed. Her question seemed too obvious to take seriously. I'd opened up and she'd responded with cheap pop psychology.

We were both quiet for a minute. The soft wind from the window felt cooler now and had the smell of rain on it. When I looked up, she seemed to be lost in recollection of something – the something, I guessed, that had happened earlier. I imagined some upstanding guy out in the town, someone with a normal life, some passion, weekends away, whatever it is people do when they are not dying.

'Actually,' I said, 'I wouldn't much care if I died right now. You know, cut myself open, watch as the nurses scramble around me, struggling to patch me up.'

She looked at me for a moment, considering what I'd just told her. Once a decent enough time had lapsed, she changed the subject, 'Last time you started telling me about Sarah.'

I didn't answer. I closed my eyes, waiting for the current.

'Barry? Do you want to tell me more about Sarah or her family?'

'Oh yes, that...' I said. 'I remember meeting them for a braai at the Rondebosch tennis club. She and her parents played. Her brother, the mama's boy, was too much of a wimp. I remembered rocking up in my fake leather jacket and an old pair of Docs.'

I took a deep breath. She nodded.

'I felt so out of place with her dad and all his posh English friends. They were all in white. Sarah had played a match that afternoon.'

The current began to get stronger. I looked past my therapist. 'When she finally got off the court I told her I had to speak to her alone.'

I was looking at the wall now, one with the current.

'I took her to one of the storerooms at the back of the clubhouse and fucked her against the wall. I fucked her hard in that sweaty white tennis dress of hers. She started crying.'

A voice in my head told me to stop, that I was going too far, being too cruel, but I kept on anyway.

'She was bleeding. I got her some tissues, but she wouldn't even look at me. So I left her there and went home and got trashed. It was the first time we'd done it. Hell, maybe it was her first time altogether. She was so damn innocent.'

When I finally looked up, her large brown eyes were inscrutable.

I looked back down at the table. My breathing was slowing again, The wave inside me was receding.

'And what happened then?' she asked.

'Oh, I stayed away for a while. Didn't hear from her. But then one day I went back to their place with the mama's boy. He wanted to show me some high-tech headset he'd got for his computer. Afterwards, I went looking for her. Found her sitting in the garden. I asked whether she was okay. Said I was sorry. But she ignored me, just stroked their old black Labrador, didn't even look at me.'

'And was that the end?'

'No.'

She waited for me to say more.

'I know what you think. You think I should hold on to the hope. As if I can ever get out of here, ever be healthy again. As if I can go back to that place and fix it all. But that's precisely the problem. To you that kind of talk makes sense. But you've just come from hell-knows-where and probably have drinks lined up at some nice restaurant later, while I come from a ward where I lay waiting for this nonsense all day, trying to fight off one spell of nausea after the other. You think hope is going to do me any good?'

'I don't know, Barry,' she said. 'You tell me.' She suddenly sounded unsure of herself. A tiny muscle below her eye began to twitch. 'What is this Barry? What is going on?'

'Don't you get it? It doesn't fucking matter!' I shouted. 'The game is up anyway.' And then, softer, 'Are we done yet?'

'Of course. We're done, if you want to be,' she said softly.

When I reached the door I glanced back. She was staring after me, her eyes large, stunned.

She shouldn't have come here. She should have just stayed in town, where she could get her lipstick smeared and her hair dishevelled and whatever else. It's not fair that she should sit here smelling like a woman, bringing the outside world in with her.

Does she not understand what torture it is for the dead to

watch the living? Couldn't she see that life was over for me? That Sarah was in the past? That she too was in the past even as she sat there? Couldn't she see that there could be no way back for me?

Back in the ward I lay on my bed and closed my eyes, my heart still pounding wildly. I tried to relax. Around me the hospital was hushed. Just another afternoon.

'Fuck!' I cursed out loud.

From his side of the ward, Jonathan cursed back. I cursed louder. He cursed back at me. I cursed again, now shouting. He burst out laughing. I told him to fuck off, but for the first time in weeks I was glad to have him there.

'Had a bad date, sport?' he asked. 'You have no idea.'

SOMETHING VERY ODD HAPPENED last night. I woke from a deep sleep to a commotion in the corridor. Someone whispered, 'Keep it down, man. You'll spook the patients.' I heard the squeak of a gurney being pushed past our door. A second voice whispered back, asking something about a mortuary.

In my drowsy state, I thought it was Von Hansmeyer, but it couldn't have been him. He is never here at night. Dugan, perhaps? I was awake now. I waited. I heard a door open much further away. Someone coughed. I wouldn't have been the only patient to be lying awake. Did someone else hear it too?

Did I imagine the whole thing? I closed my eyes to go back to sleep. Then, just as I felt my shoulders relaxing, my breathing slow, I heard a car start up. My whole body tensed up again. I threw off the sheet and rushed over to the window. In the moonlight I saw an ambulance passing through the gate. Slowly it crawled up the ridge until all I could see was two small, red lights.

Why are they taking out stiffs in the middle of the night? Why not keep it down in the mortuary and take it away in the morning? It made no sense. I felt both dizzy and scared. The previous evening's pills hadn't worn off yet. I lay back down on the snowy landscape of my bed.

I wondered who might have died. I imagined different people's bodies laid out on the stretcher. Jonathan, Espoir, Kagiso, Von Hansmeyer, my own. What's that they say about the only way out?

I repeated the whisper I had heard, 'You'll spook the patients.' And then I felt a shaking laughter growing from the pit of my stomach. Did they really think we'd be spooked? Didn't they know that we were as good as dead already, that we already knew that the credits had rolled for us, that we were just waiting for someone to turn on the lights and tell us to leave?

But then they were from the other world. The one where people cough only occasionally, where they aren't trapped in scrap-metal bodies, waiting to be recycled.

I lay for a long time listening, but there was nothing more. I eventually heard Jonathan shifting in his bed and guessed that it must almost be morning. I tried to sleep. As I finally drifted off, I made a mental note to investigate the mysterious whispers once I had managed to get some uninterrupted sleep.

When I woke it was already late morning. At first the events of the night seemed like a dream, but then I remembered watching the ambulance cross the ridge. 'Spooked?' What could that mean? Were they hiding something? Why would one more body spook us?

I rushed down to breakfast without washing my face. I had to get there before anyone left. As I entered the large room I started counting heads, faces. They all seemed to be there, no obvious absences. But then I realised how stupid I was. Being absent from the breakfast table meant nothing. A person might be in emergency or just too sick to come to breakfast. And, besides, it was already hard keeping up with the fast turnover of patients in this place. How could I find a missing person if I didn't know everyone to start with?

Deflated, I found a seat. The clever gang was discussing the droughts in the United States. Apparently civil unrest was breaking out because people in the South were beginning to starve. 'Good Christian, white-skinned Americans shooting each other,' Morris said, raising a few eyebrows at the next table. 'You can't believe what a lack of food and water does to that wholesome American spirit. Hundreds of Americans dead on the street.'

'Hillary lost control a long time ago,' Jonathan scoffed. 'The whole country is now nothing but army and private contractors protecting the rich. And as long as they have these droughts and floods, nothing will change. All downhill from here, my friends. Downhill, I tell you.'

Across the dining hall I saw Kagiso and Sibu gesticulating wildly in what I took to be a playful sparring. Like me, they didn't know or care about the outside world. Their banter ended with Kagiso pretending to punch his sidekick on the arm, at which Sibu stepped back and dragged his finger across his neck, nodding slowly and then bursting into laughter.

No one gave any indication they knew about the previous night's death, or whatever it was. Just another day in quarantine. I thought of telling the gang about it, but I figured they'd write me off as imagining things.

The only person I could think of who wasn't in the hall was the man with the scar, the one I had seen from the window while waiting for Van Vuuren. Looking back, it seems strange that I should have pinpointed him specifically – surely there were others who weren't accounted for? Yet I thought of him, and when I looked for him I couldn't see him.

I never did see the man with the scar again. It was only that once, looking down at him from the window, clouds threatening overhead. When I eventually did ask about him, no one knew whom I was talking about. 'Don't know anyone like that,' they'd say, shaking their heads. Even Jonathan, who knew everyone, didn't know whom I meant.

All I know is that I'm sure I had seen him. What happened to the guy is anyone's guess.

After breakfast I went back up and searched the corridor that led past our ward. I was still uneasy. I don't know what

I was hoping to find, maybe a telltale bloodstain, or a trail of stretcher tracks in the dust that would lead me to the hidden corner where the ghastly thing had happened.

I was about to quit, when, where the corridor turned at a right angle I spotted an angular black mark shaped like the blade of one of those Arab knives. I kneeled down. It was dark, only about ten centimetres in length. Old blood? Blood that someone had half-heartedly wipe away in the dark? As I bent my face down to the ground, the tang of iron hit me between the eyes. No doubt it was blood. I felt light-headed.

I thought of asking Von Hansmeyer about it, but as soon as the thought crept into my mind, I realised it would lead nowhere. For all his Médecins Sans Frontières goodwill and optimism, he would never tell. Whatever it is, he must be in on it. Besides, they just didn't talk about the dead.

So I scouted out what everyone in the hospital was doing. I heard Von Hansmeyer's voice booming in one of the downstairs wards. Dugan was filling in forms outside the pharmacy. Good. Very good. There was only one duty nurse on the upper level. So I strolled off to what I knew would be Von Hansmeyer's empty office, as if it was the most natural thing in the world.

At his door I stopped. I looked around. His office was in the quieter administrative wing of the hospital. I would certainly be asked what I was doing here if someone spotted me. My heart beat like the timer on an oldstyle bomb, the type you see in B-grade movies filled with suspense and action and drama, just waiting to detonate inside my chest. By now, my lungs were struggling with the effort of all the morning's walking. What the hell did I think I was doing?

I turned the shiny bronze handle. To my surprise, it gave. I pushed the door open, stumbled in, and shut it quietly behind me.

It took a minute for my eyes to get used to the gloominess of the room. After the bright white of the corridor, Von Hansmeyer's office seemed dim and stuffy. The only light came from the window filtered by a heavy grey curtain hanging in long, vertical folds to the floor. The carpeting, too, was a shade lighter than ash.

As with my previous visit, the office felt as if it could be in Sandton or Newlands. It felt as though if I opened the door again, I would emerge in a busy corporate corridor with large windows overlooking a bustling city street. All that was missing was the noise, the sounds that would have characterise such a place. There was no hum of traffic here, no far-off car alarms or vendors shouting, just a deep and heavy silence.

As my eyes grew accustomed to the dim light, I stepped over to his desk and started sifting through the stacks of papers. A basket on one corner held his mail, while a pile of papers relating to hospital supplies lay in front of his chair, a pen on top of it. I took great care to replace everything I touched exactly as it was. Still, when I put the pen back on top of the pile of papers, I wasn't sure if it had lain with the tip facing toward or away from his chair.

I'd assumed that any paperwork relating to the hapless soul who had died the previous night would be lying on his desk or on the top of a pile. But there were no other papers. I hesitated with the desk drawers. That would be crossing one line too many. I went over to the large filing cabinet instead, and slid open one of the drawers. It was stuffed with yellow paper files labelled with the names of patients.

I couldn't help but scan them for my own name. My heart was beating even faster now. I thought I heard something on the other side of the door. I froze, the hairs on my arms rising, a sweat breaking out in my neck and forehead. I held my breath, eyes fixed on the handle. All I heard, was that deep, all-pervading silence.

As I stood watching the door, it dawned on me that he must keep a list of everyone in the hospital and everyone who has died. And that list must be somewhere. Surely if I could find this list and take a look at the last entry, the mystery would be solved.

Instead, I looked back down – straight at a file labelled 'James, Barry Wilbert'.

Making a careful note that it lay between 'Jacobs' and 'Johannes', I lifted it out and flipped it open. It contained an envelope with X-rays and a small bundle of papers, some stapled together, some loose.

The top page contained a list of personal details under my name and identification number. I was startled by, 'Admitted: 2 October 2019.' Had it really been three years? I should have been either dead or back on the outside already. Under 'Diagnosis', it stated, 'Pulmonary nodulosis, third-degree resistance.' And then there was a row of boxes still not checked or filled in: 'Expelled', 'Date of death', and so on.

I turned the page to find long columns of medical jargon written in Von Hansmeyer's forceful hand. Paging through more indecipherable scribbling, near the back I found a page headed 'Serious incidents'.

'9 November 2022: Attempted suicide. Mr James was found unconscious, suspected to have jumped from a second-floor balcony. No serious injuries. Put under close observation by staff. Psychological report requested from Ms L van Vuuren.'

And when I turned the page, there it was.

'Preliminary psychological report. Patient: James, Barry. Consulting psychologist: Ms L van Vuuren. Mr James exhibits a variety of depressive symptoms, indicative of chronic depression. A positive diagnosis of clinical depression is made. Mr James also shows signs of psychosis and delusional thinking – known psychological side effects of his current nodulosis treatment regimen. A treatment switch should be considered if possible. It is, however, unlikely that the suicide attempt was directly related to his psychosis – the cause is almost certainly his severe state of depression. Due to the recent suicide attempt and continued suicidality, it is recommended that he be kept under close observation until further notice. It is also recommended that he undergoes at least one session of psychological counselling per week. Mirtazapine (30 mg daily) was prescribed (consulting psychologist to be contacted in case of nonavailability of the drug).'

Her signature below was small and neat.

I considered Van Vuuren's words for a moment. Apparently, I was now not only a patient suffering from the bug, but also a mental case. I was going psycho.

I turned the page to find the heading 'Patient history'. Just as I was about to read, I heard footsteps and voices from the corridor. This time it was for real. I closed the file, slid it back between 'Jacobs' and 'Johannes', and stood watching the door. I didn't know what to do.

So I just stood there, hands hanging at my sides, nowhere to hide.

The door handle turned. The door slowly swung into the room. It stopped about halfway and I heard Von Hansmeyer say, 'Very well, very well' to someone walking away.

Then, finally, he stood in the doorway. He fixed his small, dark eyes on me. His cheeks looked particularly ruddy, enhanced by the immaculate whiteness of his coat. He stood staring at me for a moment, his head cocked to the side. He didn't seem surprised at all. I imagined that he was calculating various scenarios, looking for the one that would deal with the situation most quickly and efficiently.

'Mr James,' he said, 'you were looking for something?'

'My file,' I said.

He closed the door behind him and slowly slipped off his coat, hanging it on a hook behind the door. He walked around the far side of his desk to his chair. As he lowered himself into it, he looked at me and said, 'Please. Have a seat, Barry.'

He took a pair of spectacles from his shirt pocket and balanced them on his nose. He looked down at his pen, a slight frown starting to crease his forehead. It was gone as soon as it was formed, passing over his face like a charge of submerged electricity.

I sat down and waited for him to speak. But he just sat there tapping his fingers. It was as if he was looking, but not seeing. The faint light from the window fell on his face and suddenly there seemed to be something misshapen about him, as if the contours of his face had shifted.

Eventually he bent down and felt for something in a desk drawer. Then he straightened up and flipped the lid off a pill box. I watched him dig out a large white pill with his index finger.

'Take this,' he said and leaned across the desk to hand it to me.

The pill felt heavy in my hand, unlike any I had ever taken. I looked up at him and he nodded, so I put the pill on my tongue and swallowed it dry.

'You know, Barry,' he sighed, 'sometimes things are not what they seem. You think you are doing one thing but you are really doing something very different. When I came to South Africa thirty-three years ago, I thought I was going to make a difference. That was 1989, Barry. Were you even born then? Do you know what this place looked like then?

'I was a young man. And now, here I am, sitting in this office in a hospital that is running out of money and where the patients make themselves comfortable in your office and smile like dumb chickens when you catch them. In thirty-three years, Barry, nothing has changed. It has just been one mess after the other. But look at me, Barry.' I looked at him, but found it hard to focus on the figure on the other side of what now seemed to be a very large desk. 'You see, Barry, I am still here. I'm not running away. I'm not going back to Hamburg. I'll keep on until the day they lower me into this hard earth of yours.'

I wanted to tell him that I couldn't quite see, that I was feeling a little drowsy and couldn't quite follow him. But when I tried to talk, my jaw was too heavy and I just sat there, waiting for him to go on.

'You see, Barry, people in this country are lazy. They expect everything to fall into their laps. The premier comes here and asks me why there is a white man in charge. He doesn't even come inside to see what we've done. He just stands there and tells me that this place isn't what he expected and then he drives away.

'But I've seen men like him. They come and go, Barry. That's why I say we have two kinds of men: those who do things, who fight on no matter what, and those who just take what they can get and fall apart as soon as things get hard. I will fight, Barry, that is how I am. And you, you are letting yourself go; you are choosing to be the other kind of man. You have no backbone. You are choosing to sit around waiting to die and leave it to others to clean up after you. You have to pull yourself together, Barry.'

My eyelids had drooped closed by now, but his words registered, almost as if they had been uttered by a demon somewhere inside my own head. Maybe he was right. Maybe I had no backbone. I forced my eyes open and saw that he was standing. Behind him the light had dimmed, reflecting eerily off his spectacles. For a moment there seemed to be something supernatural about him, something deeply disconcerting.

'You are not to come here again, Barry, unless you are invited by me personally. If you want to know something, you ask me. You do not sneak around like a thief. I will not stand for it. Whatever you were before you came here, I do not care. Here you will behave yourself.'

I felt a heaviness in the pit of my stomach. I wanted to cry, to beg his forgiveness, to say sorry, beg him to help me fight the good fight.

I remember him stepping away from the window and coming toward me, something shiny resting in his right palm. Then the tiredness became too much. I must have blacked out right there.

When I awoke, I was back in the ward, clean and white, with bright sunlight streaming in through the window. A terrible headache was throbbing in my left temple and an immense weariness weighed down my limbs. Through the loud, wind-like ringing in my ears I could hear Jonathan moving about. I croaked something. He came over to my bed.

'Had us worried there, sport,' he said. 'You been out for almost a day and a half.'

'How did I get here?' I asked.

'A nurse found you by the storerooms, lying in your own vomit. They had you in emergency for observation, but sent you back here because everything seems normal. Apart from you sleeping like a bear, of course.'

'Something strange is going on, Jonathan,' I said. 'I don't know what – they are hiding it from us – but something really bad is happening. We need to get the fuck out of here; if your plans are still, I mean, if we're still…'

'Hey!' he said, holding a finger up to his lips, his eyes darting toward the closed door. 'Take it easy, sport. You don't want to tell the whole world our secrets.'

'You're not listening. There is something bad happening. There was a corpse.'

He sighed impatiently. 'And where exactly did you see this corpse?' he asked.

And I didn't know what to say since I never actually saw a corpse; I just heard the voices and saw the ambulance driving away.

'Ah, get some rest sport,' he said and tapped me on the knee. 'Can I get you anything? Von Hansmeyer said I should let him know when you've come around.'

I felt a chill, and remembered Von Hansmeyer's office, a flash, a sense that there had been a third person in that room. Slowly the memories of our chat came back to me. Had there been someone else besides Von Hansmeyer?

And then I had a vision of a sheet of paper being put in front of me to sign. Was this a memory, or was I imagining it? It didn't fit anywhere, but it seemed so real.

'Anything wrong, sport?' Jonathan asked from the door, something close to concern now on his face.

'I don't know.

When I finally managed to pull myself out of bed and took a shower, my body felt bloated and lumpy under the cold water. But standing under the pounding jet of that icy water I suddenly felt better. I was washing something off. Whatever had happened the previous evening, whatever dreadful death awaited me here, I felt as if I was washing it all off me, the accumulated dirt of many months in this place.

When I was done, I heard someone coughing in the dressing area. As I rounded the corner, I saw Sibu bent over, hacking up a slimy, yellow goo into a wad of toilet paper. He seemed very frail, little more than a skeleton of a man in a grubby towel. He saw me and turned around. His scrawny shoulders tensed and rippled. He winked at me. 'Mechanic says you're joining us. Better be ready, white boy.'

'I'll be ready,' I said and winked back. I was relieved that Jonathan had not cut me out of the escape plans. I had expected him to write me off after our disagreement out in the back yard.

When I got back to the ward, Jonathan was out. Feeling more refreshed than I had in a long time, I pulled my chair up to the window and opened it wide. It was late afternoon and the worst of the day's heat had dissipated. I let the cool air flow over my newly cleaned body.

I reached out to take a notebook from the drawer, to write a note of my visit to Von Hansmeyer's office. But the notebooks weren't where I left them. The top drawer was empty. In a panic I flung open all the drawers. It flashed through my mind that they may have been confiscated. Von Hansmeyer? Van Vuuren? Dugan even?

And then, there they were, neatly stacked in the bottom drawer, pencils lined up alongside. Relief flooded through my body, numbing the receptors in my nerve ends. Even though I knew from the start that I wouldn't be able to hide them or lock them up, I had fooled myself into thinking they'd be safe. I thought of Von Hansmeyer and imagined him sitting in his dusty little office peering at my crooked handwriting through his little round spectacles. Maybe he wanted me to know that my papers weren't safe either, that he could go through my thoughts as well. Well, screw you, Von Fucking Hansmeyer. I'll show you what s going on in my head – and you'll wish you never looked. To hell with it, I thought.

I sat for a while, fuming, watching the guard out there in his little guard tower by the gate. He seemed to be busy with something, constantly on the move, up and down, hands busy. Standing with phone in hand, then disappearing out of sight for a moment, then reappearing and bending over to write something. What kept him so damn busy? Apart from the comings and goings of the staff, he hardly have anything to do.

Okay then, I thought, I'd write not for myself, but for whoever would read it. Nothing would be private any more. Something deep inside me realigned that day, something to do with the loss of privacy, the white pill, the shower, the plans to escape. I felt that my life was on a new trajectory, that in one elegant twist of fate all had changed. I started imagining that someone would one day read all this, someone like Sarah, or whoever. That is why I could keep on with it, why it became an obsession, why I'm sitting here now, months later, filling page after page of this notebook. Let them have it. Let them have it all.

I WOKE UP THE next morning feeling better than I'd felt in a long time. After a large breakfast, including two cups of coffee, I went for a walk around the hospital and then returned to the ward to write. As I sat down, I wondered whether the pill Von Hansmeyer had given me wasn't behind this sea change, cleaning me up from inside. Maybe it was some new drug they were testing that made you vomit and cough out all the bad, leaving you with only the good, cleaner and healthier. It was as if a fog had lifted from my mind, as if I could see the world more clearly.

As I sat at the window, a small silver Hyundai crossed the ridge and snaked its way down to the gate. When it stopped, a red-haired woman in a blue summer dress got out and walked over to the guardhouse. She waved and said something to the guard and his broad bestubbled smile was visible all the way from where I was sitting.

She didn't look up once on her way to the front door of the hospital. I watched her walk with a briskness that seemed to have something irrepressibly optimistic about it. I imagined I could smell the sweet spice of her perfume rising up from her bare shoulders.

Seeing her bursting with life like that tugged at some

submerged part of me. Yet, I saw clearly that I had to leave that part of me behind, cut the line that held me here, shed the notion like an old skin. It was all so terribly predictable. Here I was, isolated and sick, and I was attaching myself to a person, a living, vibrant person. It could have been anyone. Anyone could have brought those shape-shifting colours of life into the hospital...

But those colours were an illusion – to me anyway. If they meant something to someone, it would be to the man or woman who had smudged her lipstick like that. Let them have the life I can't.

'Let me be. Do not tempt me with life when I am already detaching my spirit from this fragile mess.'

And, as she passed out of sight, I felt a further weight lifting. Once again I felt clean, as if all had been stripped away from me, as if I'd washed the world away. The more I focused on that sense of freedom, that letting go, the purer it became. In my mind's eye I saw the white pill, huge, as if suspended far above the desert sand. It became a beacon to me, a guide by which I could find my way out of the chaotic world around me.

I WAS STANDING IN the back yard, looking out over the deadness of the veld beyond the fence. Jonathan stood next to me, his gaunt face at once serious and yet without any sign of tension. I felt as if we should have had cigarettes in our hands, staring out between clouds of smoke, actors in an old black-and-white movie, waiting for the credits to roll.

'So, boss, how we busting out of this place?' I asked.

'Patience, sport,' he said, and glanced around to make sure we were alone. A few other patients were sitting on a bench a stone's throw away. Satisfied that we were out of earshot, he turned to me.

'Well, firstly, it it's not just the four of us. Kagiso had an attack of conscience or something. I can't make sense of him, but I won't complain. Maybe they are hoping we will divert the police's attention away from them once we're on the outside.'

'Morris?'

'Yes, and Adams. And then three of Kagiso's buddies. Makes nine of us. A bit much, but there you go.'

Jonathan turned around. We walked along the fence to the furthest corner of the yard. 'I was at the management meeting this morning. From next month, they are starting to cut the staff by thirty per cent. Going to hit the night staff mainly. There will be one guard in the tower and just two others: one in the control room and another patrolling. Oh, and only two nurses on duty in the evenings.'

He stopped and turned to me. 'How does that sound, sport?'

'Sounds better than seven or eight pairs of eyes, I suppose,' I said. 'But it still won't be easy. You know as well as I that security is not as lame as it was before.'

'Of course it won't be easy. But with one guard in the tower and another with us, we only really have one guard to worry about.'

'Yes,' I nodded and we started walking again.

'So, sport, we are talking about next month some time. Exactly when will depend on the new work rosters. We got lucky, our man on the inside is staying on and should be on duty a few times next month. We still have to figure out exactly how we're going to punch a hole, but our man should have control over the lights back here, as well as the current in the fence.'

We reached the far corner of the yard and again stood staring out. 'Do we know what's out there?' I asked, not expecting an answer. 'Not really,' he said. And then after a long pause, 'Maybe that's something you can help us with. You know the library better than I do. Maybe there's a map we can use.'

'Sure, I'll take a look. But we don't have a getaway car or anything like that, do we?'

'No,' he said. 'Kagiso was very clear about that. Once we are on the other side of the fence, we are on our own. That's why I think they may be hoping we'll be some kind a diversion, distract the guards while they make their getaway. They might even be counting on us getting caught. We'll just have to hope we can get far enough away before anyone notices.'

We had now reached the opposite corner of the yard. I stood looking at the pole I had marked a few weeks previously. 'Are we actually going to be on the other side of this fence?' I said, again not expecting an answer.

'It won't be easy sport, but yes.'

For whatever reason, I felt myself smiling. Jonathan winked.

I turned and looked back at the hospital. I froze. Side by side in a second-floor window across the courtyard I saw Von Hansmeyer and Van Vuuren. They were looking straight at us. I shivered.

'Barry?' Jonathan said.

'Don't look,' I said. 'We're being watched.'

He turned and followed my gaze. He looked straight back at them.

Then, after a pause, he lifted his right hand and waved. Only Ms Van Vuuren lifted her hand and waved back feebly.

Von Hansmeyer and I stood perfectly still. I felt his eyes resting on me across what must have been more than fifty metres. It was as if he were reaching inside me, those large fingers of his groping around for my heart, or whatever you choose to call the essence that keeps a man going. I felt as though he knew all about me, every word I had just spoken to Jonathan.

Then again, maybe he just wanted his pill back.

marginalia

A T THIS POINT IN James's journals, two entirely unrelated points become clear, the first a reflection of the times in which he found himself, particularly the socio-political milieu of the years following the outbreak of the plague, and the second offering some insight into the psyche of Barry James himself.

Firstly, in February 2022, South Africa's national health service was crippled by a series of nationwide strikes. The strikes were triggered by the non-payment of overtime and what the Democratic Nursing Union of South Africa described as 'years of underinvestment in human resources' and 'untenable working conditions'. The strikes eventually led to the dismissal of Minister of Health Dr Benny Malakoane – and some critics argue that it was also a turning point in the presidency of Dr Zwai Mkhize.

While an agreement between government and the unions meant that staff at Pearson and at the seven other quarantine facilities in the Great Karoo did not take part in the strike, staff from these facilities were redeployed to make up for shortages elsewhere in the health service. The information regarding reduced staff levels related by Fox, via James, roughly corresponds with records kept by the Eastern Cape Department of Health. Further access to these records is restricted.

The second issue raised by James's notes thus far is open to further analysis, but provides some clue as to the inner workings of Mr James's mind, how he views his world, and not only how that emerged in his writing, but also how it developed over time, depending for the most part on circumstance – his notions of both freedom and resignation, and how these fluctuated over the time he spent journalling.

Throughout the journals it is clear that Mr James is preoccupied with colour and light. His notes refer to shades and shadow throughout, his observations astute, almost haunting. He draws constant parallels between light and dark, giving them meaning and nuance. He notes, for instance, that Ms Van Vuuren brings 'shape-shifting colours' into the Pearson facility; he emphasises the whiteness of the pill given to him by Von Hansmeyer, the redness of Van Vuuren's hair, and the shades of the land and sky at various times of day and in varying weather conditions. This contrasts starkly with his insistence on the greyness and blandness of his world, drawing analogies, almost as if intentionally highlighting the contrasts of his inner and outer world.

'I SAW YOU STANDING outside with your friend yesterday,' she said, her voice more businesslike than usual. 'Is he your roommate?' She had come in with the same briskness I'd seen before, on her way from her car to the hospital entrance. Her hair was tied neatly behind her head, and the mask she wore looked brand new. She was nothing like the flushed, dishevelled girl of our previous meeting.

'Yes, he is. We saw you too.'

'Sorry, I guess we were spying.'

'That's okay,' I said. 'I did some spying of my own.'

'Doctor Von Hansmeyer told me,' she said, smiling with her eyes.

'Of course he did. That is just like the bastard.'

'He's not that bad, you know. He doesn't have to do this. He could quite easily go back to Europe and have a very comfortable life in Germany. Instead, he struggles away down here, working for next to nothing. He's one of the good guys.'

'Good guys?'

Behind her, the window was closed. The day had turned blustery.

Earlier that morning, when I had sat staring out of my

window in the ward, it had seemed sunny and quiet. Now the clouds had drifted in like an afternoon headache.

'Have you thought any more about what we spoke about last time?' she asked. There was a weary undertone in her voice.

'Yes, I suppose I think about that stuff all the time,' I said. 'I guess I got a bit carried away. I'm sorry if I... if I went a bit too far. It's just so hard to explain what it's like in here, though. I'm not sure I could ever get it across.'

'That's okay, Barry,' she said, her voice a gentle nail scratching at my dead heart. 'Of course I can't understand, but I'll try, Barry.'

We were quiet again. The wind tugged at the windowpane, rattling it in its frame, letting the reflected light play against the far wall. Barely audible noises drifted in from deep inside the hospital. I looked past her at the bank of grey clouds beyond the window. Then I looked straight into her big, brown eyes and she looked straight back at me. Maybe because of my apology, maybe just because I had let my guard down, we had reached some kind of stasis, a ledge on a rocky slope. Any further talk could dislodge everything and send us on our separate ways.

'As I told you, Sarah's parents had a house in Rondebosch,' I said. 'She and her brother were watching it one holiday. I remember standing in their garden and feeling so terribly out of place in that world. You know Rondebosch... tall trees, thick, cool grass, large houses, families. I went inside and she was on this white leather couch reading a book, the leaves throwing moving shadows on her hair. She read me a Keats poem then... I don't remember the poem, but I remember how I felt. I still think of that sometimes – quite often, actually.

'So she let you back in?'

'Oh, she was different to before, cold. Wouldn't let me touch her at all, clearly didn't want me there. But eventually she stopped ignoring me. I'd sit down next to her and she'd read whatever she was reading aloud to me. She even read to me from the Bible once. She started asking me to do things for her, to go to the shop to buy her some of that fancy chocolate she liked, things like that. She never mentioned what happened – not to me, probably not to anyone.'

'Did she have friends?'

'She had the kind of friends someone like her has. Anyway, they never stayed long when I was there. Or if they were going to stay, then I didn't.'

Outside the wind had picked up even more. The window rattled violently. Ms Van Vuuren went over to it to fasten the latch more tightly. For a moment she was perfectly framed, a silhouette, a dark flame.

'I used to think I was in love with her, you know. Sarah, I mean,' I continued. 'But now I know I just wanted their life. I was in love with their world, their BMWs and black Labradors, her stupid innocence. I wanted to fit in. Never mind if she treated me like a leper, I'd keep going back; every opportunity I got I'd go to their house. It felt like my one shot at another life.'

'What was wrong with your life? Surely they and their lives weren't better than yours?'

'Maybe she, they, were actually better than me. Anyway, that's not what it's about… It was a chance for a different kind of life, a chance to do it right, to get it right. But what does it matter now? I blew my hand and she's gone.'

'I could bring you some Keats, if you like, if that would mean something to you,' she said.

'No, I'm done with all that bullshit.'

'But why?'

'Because that life is over. It's a million miles away, even though it feels like it is right here.'

'It must be hard for you to have lost all that,' she said. I sensed she was taking advantage of my candour to push a little further, dig a little deeper. I didn't object, but I did feel our connection starting to slip.

'Yes, it was hard,' I said.

In the long silence that followed I felt myself drifting away from her.

We were in the same dusty room, but our lives, our prospects were so far apart. I suddenly felt terribly, terribly sad.

That evening I lay on my bed, unable to get Sarah out of my mind. Fragments of memory kept drifting into my consciousness – the day she had read me that poem; other days, at the beach, or at a braai at her brother's apartment block after watching the rugby on television.

Sarah, here in this place where men cough themselves to death while I lie awake. Sarah in this dark, rotting hellhole. Sarah, wandering around like a ghost among wounded soldiers. Sarah, dead to me, but still in the room… Sarah, haunting my every hour simply because the dead cannot help but haunt the living.

IN THE RUINS OF an old house I lay my head
By the soft morning to rise
Not to move but to stare
To feel the dust upon my skin
To watch the redness of the world and to wait
For I knew
That soon enough the smell of dust would turn to death
That I'd see her sitting
A skeleton with threaded hairs of dusty sunlight
Or maybe a figure on the ridge in the late afternoon
Stumbling toward me with no purpose
But come to judge

To CALL IT A library would give you the wrong idea. It was no more than an abandoned storeroom in a neglected part of the hospital. It had shelving on two sides, three hard chairs, a large wooden table in the middle and a row of overflowing boxes against the far wall. It was full of books. The better books weighed down heavily on the shelves. The boring books we kept in the boxes. Other books were stacked on the floor against every inch of open wall.

As with so many other good things in the hospital – Jonathan's spot on the management committee, our *Sunday Times* subscription – the library suddenly materialised after that first escape. People were happy for us to be locked up, but needed their consciences soothed. So they sent us books to keep us busy. Unfortunately, most of the boxes that arrived contained the sort of thing unlikely to raise much interest among a bunch of sick men grappling with their own everyday reality, mostly romance novels and Christian self-help books. Maybe the outside world thought that all we needed was romance and religion. Maybe they thought that would cure us of the sin that made us sick in the first place.

I had volunteered to help sort the stacks of donated books.

We didn't have a librarian or anything like that. It was strictly a library for and by the patients. Well, considering the selection of books, maybe not quite for the patients.

Either way, I spent a lot of time down there in those days. Partly because something about the dusty air in that old storeroom-cum-library and the smell of books reminded me of Sarah, but also because I started reading and discovered, to my surprise, that I actually liked it. I never got into all those romance and 'Let God into your life' nonsense. But I didn't have to. Between all the junk there were two boxes with badly drawn wineglasses and the words 'Handle with care' on them. Inside these were the treasures of our collection: some space westerns, some crime novels, some slightly tedious Penguin classics and some grim Russian authors I rather took to.

They weren't the kind of books Sarah would read, admittedly. She was all Keats and chick lit. But sitting there reading through all those months nevertheless felt a little like I was spending time with her. Actually, it felt like hanging out in her untouched room after she had died. It may sound disturbed, but there was something calming about imagining that she had just died and that I was hanging out in her room, something that helped me forget that I was in the middle of nowhere, waiting to die myself.

I didn't have much hope of finding the map Jonathan had asked me for. I knew our small collection pretty well and I'd never seen a map book or travel guide. Maps weren't exactly the kind of thing do-gooders would have sent us. It was not as if we'd be going on sightseeing trips anytime soon.

Still, after some hours of sorting through the boxes of junk, I found a book about the xerophytes of the Karoo. I had been paging through in the hope of identifying the ugly scrub scattered around the front of the hospital, when I stumbled upon a map. It wasn't very detailed, just major roads and towns, but I figured it would do.

Back in the ward, I found Jonathan asleep, which was unusual because he never slept in the day time – a fear of missing out on the goings-on, I suspect. Yet here he was, head back, eyes closed, face shrunken. I watched him lying there, a frown etched on his forehead, as if he was having an unnerving dream, perhaps a nightmare about the end of the world. Every now and again he caught his breath and snorted. I left the book on his bedside table and lay down for a nap myself.

When I woke, Jonathan had made himself comfortable in the chair next to my bed. 'Look at this sport,' he said. 'Perdetanne.'

'Perdetande,' he said again, drawing the syllables out, taking pleasure from his inability to pronounce the Afrikaans word. With a flourish he turned the open book to me. There was a picture of a small, otherworldly plant with narrow white flowers. The subscript read: 'Perdetande (horse teeth) – *Haworthia truncate*.'

'I was wondering about that,' I yawned. 'There is one just like it out back.'

'Really?' he said, genuinely surprised.

'You see the map?'

'Yes. Thanks, sport. Good work.'

He twisted his neck to peer around the door, then whispered. 'Slight spot of bother, sport. Our guard doesn't actually know how to work the bleeding lights. It is all automated. Kagiso says our guard is a bit thick.'

'What does that mean for us?' I said, sitting up. It was dangerous to talk in the ward. I wished he'd stop. I could tell that he wasn't going to.

'Well, Kagiso wants to blow his way out like the previous escape. He has his mind set on this coming Thursday. I tried to convince him otherwise, but I don't know… He's not thinking clearly.'

'What day is today?' I honestly didn't know. As with

everything else about the outside world, I had no use for the days of the week. I hadn't kept count for years.

'Saturday,' he said. 'Whatever happens, Barry, I'm not shooting my way out. That would be suicide.'

'We'll just have to find another way then.'

As I LAY BACK on the white, snowy sheets that night, my mind kept returning to the escape, or at least the possibility of escape. I don't think I ever considered escape an actual possibility. Until then, it was a daydream. Nothing more.

Besides, escape from what? Where would there be to go? Wasn't the whole world slowly coming apart, being scorched beyond recognition? I could escape it as little as I could escape myself, my damaged lungs, the bacteria slowly multiplying inside me.

And yet, despite all this, despite my better judgement, I felt something like excitement. Here was something taking shape, something to get carried away by. Of course, I knew I was just going along for the ride... but that in itself was something. I didn't expect to find anything out there anyway. It was the going that was the thing.

But then, as I was pondering the fence and its invisible charge of electricity, I thought of the control room and was reminded of my visit to Von Hansmeyer's office. My thoughts flittered around like that sometimes.

I hadn't thought of that strange visit much since I woke up that bleached-out morning with the wind in my ears. Whatever happened – and I was reminded of that disconcerting sense that there had been a third person standing behind me in that dim room – none of it mattered. At least not right then. It was as if there had been a turning point, as if taking that large white pill had rewound something inside me and given me a new clarity that would help me push on and beyond the cold wire of that fence.

My instinct told me not to dwell too much on the past, even the recent past, but to cling instead to the clarity offered by that white pill and to leave all confusion behind me, not to question my own motives. Just moving may have been one reason for going, but there was something more, something locked up in the mystery of the white pill. The white pill was the key, the key to getting away from it all, away from the strange light in Von Hansmeyer's office, from the man with the scar on his face.

ONCE AGAIN I WAS in the ballroom. The lavish red curtains hung draped as they had before. I was still impressed by the workmanship in the finely fluted pillars of gold still. This time, though, the room was not filled with dancers. In fact, I was quite alone.

I walked over to one of the floor-to-ceiling windows through which cold white daylight streamed into the room. I stood looking out at the falling snow. A hundred metres or so off was the beginnings of a gentle rise in the ground. And there, in a thick, dark green phalanx, loomed a thick forest of cedar. The trees stretched far up a hill to where it disappeared in the mist of the falling snow.

I remember a sense of wonder that the world could have changed that much. I didn't question it, though. I accepted the transformation of the hospital and its surroundings as simultaneously wonderful and completely unsurprising. Dare I say, my being here even had a sense of homecoming about it.

A fire crackled in a massive hearth on the far side of the ballroom. Next to it lay piles of wood in a long gold-coloured basket. Long, silver tools with which to manage the fire hung hooked over the edge of the basket.

Next thing I remember, I was standing by the fire and Ms

Van Vuuren was handing me a glass of port. 'Come on, Mr James, lighten up,' she said. She was dressed as before in bright white, her shoulders bare, long white gloves reaching past her elbows.

'You know,' she continued, her red lips twisting into a smile, 'I'm really glad to see you here. I wasn't sure you'd come.'

I assured her I wouldn't have missed it for the world. As I said this, it occurred to me that I didn't know what 'it' was. Not that it mattered, of course. I was here. She was here.

There were other people too now. Men, all men in black tuxedos, men with finely cropped hair that spoke in what I took to be Polish. Before I could answer her, one of the men took her arm and led her toward another to whom she was introduced. I watched as he bowed slightly and gently took her gloved hand to his lips and saw, too, the heart-wrenching smile she offered in return.

She stood talking with these men for a very long time, mostly just nodding and smiling as they chattered. I kept thinking that one might be the broad-shouldered nurse, Dugan, but I couldn't be sure. He did, after all, look nothing like him.

I wanted to talk to her, but she kept eluding me, avoiding my eye. Once I tried to join her circle and a large bearded man stepped in front of me, saying something in Polish which I took to mean 'You'd better stay where you are'.

I think I struggled with him, I'm not sure. But the next thing I remember I was sitting in Von Hansmeyer's office. Von Hansmeyer was behind his desk, saying something about how I had no business harassing Ms Van Vuuren. I wanted to defend myself, to explain that she was my friend, but he wouldn't listen. 'She is very traumatised,' he said. 'Very traumatised. I should be locking you up.'

Then I got that horrible feeling again that there was someone behind me. As it occurred to me, I noticed a thin smile forming on Von Hansmeyer's lips. I wanted to get up. I wanted to scream, but I couldn't. I was stuck there, paralysed.

Von Hansmeyer nodded and said something I couldn't quite make out, and then I got the sense that something was moving behind me, a shadow falling across my back.

I woke with a shake. It was still dark. It could have been any time from midnight to three o'clock, that time of night when it is impossible to tell. The faint scent of ammonia. The deep quiet of many people sleeping.

I lay for a few minutes, feeling that peculiar combination of relief and loneliness one often feels when waking after a nightmare. And then I stiffened and felt the blood drain from my face, for suddenly I knew, as clearly as one knows anything, that there had in fact been someone standing behind me in the dream. The man with the scar on his face. And that he wasn't thinking kind thoughts.

I WAS READING ONE of those trashy crime capers down in the library when a guard flung open the door and dropped the morning's *Sunday Times* on the table. He looked at me and hesitated at the door.

'It's okay,' I said. 'I'm not going to read it. I prefer my fiction on smaller pages.'

He still hovered. I nodded. I could see his mind working, his eyes narrowing. After a long, uncomfortable silence he left, pulling the door closed behind him.

I reached out and pulled the paper toward me. What the hell... I could feel an irregular shape tucked between the newsprint and, unfolding it, pulled out a thin A4 booklet with the words *R McBride Security Systems* in small, maroon letters on the cover. The manual seemed to have been custom-made for the hospital. Some pages consisted of diagrams of switches and odd words, like 'line in parabola' and 'alarm dispersal calibrator'. Apart from the unusual terminology, though, it didn't seem all that complicated.

Hardly five minutes later the door burst open and Kagiso and Jonathan marched in like cops out to apprehend a felon. Kagiso looked at me and then at Jonathan. 'What's your fucking bitch doing here?' he barked.

'Who, Barry? Barry is okay,' Jonathan said.

'This is not cool, man. This is not how we do things.' There was a cold edge to Kagiso's voice. He was speaking to Jonathan, but looking at me.

'I see you already got the paper there, old sport,' Jonathan said, trying hard to sound calm.

'Yes,' I said, 'I forgot what happy reading it makes. Famine here, war there, people being raped down the road. It's really quite something.'

'I know,' he said.

I slid the manual from under a fold of newsprint and held it out to them. Kagiso stepped toward me and yanked it out of my hand. He pulled up a chair and sat down at the table, spreading the booklet open in front of him.

We waited, watching a frown crease his forehead. Finally, I turned back to the newspaper and started reading a story about how the country's flood-preparedness plans would be completely useless if we were hit by storms similar to those that had been tormenting the east coast of the United States. One person they quoted said they wouldn't be talking about the day the levees broke, because none of the levees would have been completed. And then, right at the end of the piece, they quoted some freak who said that the warming of the planet could still be turned around and that the rising of sea levels could be reversed. Imagine that.

I was about to start reading a second story about trouble at the abandoned uranium mines just down the road from us in Beaufort West when Kagiso, now calmer, said, 'Hey, Jonathan, come over here. What does this bullshit mean?' Jonathan, who had been standing at one of the bookshelves, running his finger along the spines as though making a selection, walked over and leaned over the page. 'Hmmm...' He pulled up a chair, sat down next and paged through the manual.

Kagiso sat back, swinging his arms back and forth over the backrest. 'Shit, man, you don't have some electronics manuals around here?' he asked, looking at me as if I was the official librarian. I thought of saying I'll check our index, but I didn't.

'No, I would have known if there was.'

Hunched over the manual, Jonathan was muttering to himself. Kagiso tapped on the table with his fingers.

'You need someone who knows electronics,' I said. 'Don't you know someone, Kagiso?' I think it was the first time I had ever said his name to him. He thought for a moment.

'No... Fuck! We go through all the trouble of getting the thing and then we're too stupid to read it!' He slammed his fist on the table. 'What the fuck did you whiteys go to those fancy schools for!'

Jonathan froze.

'I'll find someone,' Jonathan said quietly.

'Someone we can trust,' Kagiso said. There was a long silence while Jonathan continued to page back and forth.

Then, quite suddenly Kagiso stood up and said, 'Fuck, pussies, I'll deal with this later,' and left.

Jonathan was as good as his word. I saw him doing the rounds in the dining hall, sitting down to chat at one table and then another. When he eventually came over to where Adams, Morris and I were finishing up the day's meatless stew, he winked at me and I knew he had found someone.

Lance Greeff had spent more than thirty years of his life laying cables for the Port Elizabeth municipality – latterly expensive fibre optics in service of their misguided attempts to turn the city into a technological hub. He was old, bony and mostly stowed away in his ward in the soon-to-be-dead wing of the hospital.

'First thing in the morning you come do a house call with me, sport,' Jonathan said. And then when I didn't answer, 'I'm not asking, I'm telling you. I'm not taking any more shit.'

The soon-to-be-dead wing of the hospital is not a place to visit. Whereas in our wing patients can still walk around, folk over there mostly lie in bed drooling and bleeding yellow pus. It is where they put elderly patients or those who come in in the advanced stages of the disease. It has only ten or fifteen rooms, but rooms through which bodies slip like ghosts through a railway station.

We found Lance Greeff lying with his eyes closed, his breathing loud and irregular, his face rubbery and dry.

Jonathan said, 'Hello, Mister Greef, sir.'

The old man's psoriatic eyelids opened slowly like that of a geriatric cat suffering from radiation sickness. A long, thick hair protruded from his nose.

Before he could say anything, a small, large-eyed man we had never seen before slid out of the adjacent bed and stepped forward, hand outstretched. We both shook his hand. He smiled toothlessly, his large eyes drifting from me to Jonathan and then back to me. His eyes rested on me with a peculiar intensity, as if he was expecting something. The freak made me feel really uneasy.

'Can't speak,' Greeff grunted. 'I think someone cut his tongue out. Sold it for muti.'

'Can you understand us?' Jonathan asked the little man.

'Only understands some Afrikaans,' said Greeff. 'I think he came from a farm around here. As far as I can tell, anyway… Their little boesman slave. You know, to shine the shoes.'

At the word 'boesman', the man's eyes darted to Greeff and then back to us.

'In this fucking day and age,' Jonathan said with what sounded like real surprise. 'What's his name?'

'Boesman.'

Boesman may have looked a little odd, with his loose-fitting standard issue, his small frame, and toothless grin, but he didn't look stupid. And the way he came forward to shake our hands and then stood up straight, looking from one to the other, had a self-assuredness one would not expect from an abused slave. He also didn't seem very sick at all, just old.

It felt wrong to me. The situation with this odd little man was too absurd. I wondered. Maybe they were about to burst out laughing, pointing their rotting fingers at us, showing us their toothless mouths. The joke would be on us.

'I understand you worked with electronics and wires and things?' Jonathan asked the man in the bed.

'You could say that. I laid cables once. Why?'

'We need you to help us make sense of some drawings.'

'Maybe. What's in it for me?' His voice was a dry monotone between raw gasps for breath. He clearly wasn't interested in what we had to say.

'What would you like to be in it?'

'Brandy.'

'I'm sure we can organise that, sir.'

'Really?' Greeff said. 'You boys can get hold of some brandy? In that case you boys have yourself a consultant.'

On the way back to our ward there was something manic about Jonathan – the wild look in his eyes, the exaggerated gestures. Maybe it was just another sign of how he was beginning to unhinge, how he was getting ready for his big exit. I had never seen him so carried away. 'We're going to do it, sport – we're going to do it.' Right there in the corridor, out loud, with no care for who's listening, 'We're going to bust out of this shithole.'

For the escape to mean anything, I had to come clean. I had to cut all ties with my hospital self. I had to let the white pill expand in the space between me and her, expand until it was the size of the sun. I had to cleanse what there was left in me to cleanse, so that I could venture into that nothingness vacant and pure.

So then, that last time in that dusty room next to Von Hansmeyer's office, we'd been talking about how the medication made me tired when she suddenly changed the subject.

'You told me about how you tried to get Sarah and her family to accept you,' she said. 'But you never finished telling me what happened. Was she still keeping you at arm's length when you got sick?' She was in a serious mood again, her hair combed back and her eyes large and quietly intense.

'There were some times. Times when I thought we were connecting... Lazy afternoons, a beach at Camps Bay on one occasion, a bookshop in Kalk Bay, that day she read me the poem, but no, no she never really let me in. I think she probably hated me.'

I looked past her, out the window. Beyond the fence the Karoo was baked dead and hard. I thought of what it would be like to be out there, and then desperately wanted to be out there. But it wasn't time yet. I couldn't leave without first breaking the chains.

'Well, actually... She said she wanted to go dancing, some place I'd go – meaning she wanted to slum it a little with white trash like me. It felt wrong right away, but I wasn't going to say no. So we went to a place I had heard of in Salt River, all flashing lights and crackhead music. She danced a lot. Guys bought her drinks. She smiled at them and hung onto their arms. It was as if I wasn't there. That is until she came stumbling toward me saying she felt sick and I should take her home. I helped her into her car and took the keys. When we got to her house she said she didn't want her father to see her in such a state.'

I looked up to see if she was listening. She nodded. I sighed. The current was weak now and I knew that soon I'd have no use for it any more.

'What made that second time worse was that I knew she didn't really want it. The months since the tennis club had made that clear. I knew that when she woke up the next morning, sober, she'd resolve never to talk to me again. I knew all that and I did it anyway. I, of course, didn't know that she'd get pregnant and swallow pills, but I knew I was fucking up...So that' it. I've regretted it so much, I'm all out of whatever it is we use when we regret things.'

'I'm so sorry, Barry,' she whispered.

'Oh, well...'

We shared another long silence. I looked out at the pale sky behind her. It seemed windy out there, as though the wind would never tire of blowing. Then I stared down at the desktop between us. I stretched out my hand and ran my finger along the small grooves in the wood.

'It was my one chance at a real life, one chance of something different... so I deserve all that's coming to me. It is my punishment. God's verdict.'

'You think God is punishing you?'

'Yes, that's why my lungs are filled with pus, why all this is here,' I indicated the hospital around me. 'The details of infection don't matter. I was judged and I deserve all that's coming to me. The end.'

There was a questioning look in her eyes, but she didn't say anything. We sat in silence for a long time. Finally, my mind drifted back to the white pill Von Hansmeyer had given me. I thought of how clean it had made me feel.

'I think I've said everything I needed to say to you,' I said. 'You can go write it all in your report now.'

'I think we have a lot more to talk about,' she said softly. 'There is a lot for you to work through.'

'I'm done working through it,' I said. 'This was it. It is over now. I can bury my secrets here with you. You can write it up as a dead man's history in your report, and I can forget all about it.'

'Barry, you have been doing very well. But you have to keep going. You can do it at your own pace, it doesn't matter. You are not to blame, Barry.'

She was trying to chain me down, to tie me to the weight I had just shrugged off. But no, I thought of that large white pill and the emptiness beyond the fence, and I felt her grip loosen, felt the chains slacken.

'I really do appreciate how you've tried to help me, but it is time for me to move on. I don't expect you to understand, but it is just the way it has to be.'

I got up and left her sitting there. It was all too easy.

For some days following that final meeting I felt strangely exposed, vulnerable even. At any moment I expected police cars to come racing over the ridge or for Von Hansmeyer to call me into his office to tell me I was being transferred. But my past didn't catch up with me. She didn't tell.

All this time I tried not to think of her. I knew that it was over, but the end had seemed so random. It had no closure to it. No dramatic exit. To hell with all of it. My business was elsewhere, in as far as I had business left in this world.

A S I PUSHED OPEN the library door, there was a rustle of activity followed by an awkward silence. Jonathan sat with the paper wide open in front of him, half obscuring the old man behind him. The old man was reading a motoring supplement folded open on the table in front of him. But from the over-elaborate way he was turning his head and letting his eyes drift from side to side, it was clear that he was pretending.

I pulled the door shut behind me and asked Jonathan how they were doing.

'Getting there,' he said.

Greeff had shifted the motoring supplement aside again and was looking down at two pages of diagrams. With a small pencil the old man had made a few notes next to the indecipherable sketches.

'I need to see the rest,' he said in a loud wheeze.

'Keep it down,' Jonathan hissed. I could see that he was nervous.

'I know it is the alarm,' the old man said. 'I am not that stupid. I know what you are doing.'

'Well, just tell us how to switch it off then,' Jonathan said.

'I'll tell you, but first I want to see the brandy.'

At this, Jonathan got up and went in search of Kagiso who had promised to get hold of some. 'Keep an eye on him, Barry,' he told me as he left. I sat listening to the old man's loud breathing. Then I picked up my crime caper and continued reading where I had left off the previous day. Sitting there reading wasn't the same with the old man there. His raspy breathing cut like a chainsaw through the silence. As in his ward, a sickly smell of stale urine hung about him like a poisoned halo.

I felt him looking at me and raised my eyes from my book. We sat looking at each other for a while. Oddly, there was nothing uncomfortable about us looking at each other like that. It felt like meeting someone I had known for years, someone with whom I was perfectly comfortable.

'You know there is nothing out there,' he said eventually, his eyes as clear as I had ever seen them. 'All of it is coming to an end.'

'I know.'

'But still you are planning to escape?'

'Yes.'

'Why?'

'It's something to do.'

'Ah. Well, we'll all soon be dead anyway. Wouldn't matter then. I thought you might have a girl you want to go see.'

'No, nothing like that.'

'If I escaped I would go see my wife in PE. Not that she'd want to see me.' He laughed as he said this, and his single nose hair quivered.

He looked back down at the papers spread out in front of him. Apparently, he had said what he wanted to. I didn't feel like reading any further, though. So I just sat there waiting for Jonathan to come back.

'This is a strange machine,' Greeff said, to himself more than to me. 'Maybe it can't be switched off.'

I didn't say anything; I just sat there watching him and

wondering how ironic it was that I was now the jailer, the one having to watch over another. Had he tried to leave, I would have stopped him. I would have stood by the door and refused to let him out. Had he shouted, I would have throttled his scrawny neck. We had embarked upon a course, and even though I had my reservations about our destination, I wasn't going to let him derail our plans.

As the light that fell through the window started to fade, I got more and more impatient. We couldn't sit here all night. We'd have to switch on the light, and then a guard or a nurse would certainly look in. They'd know something was up, at least Dugan would.

After a chapter or so of slow reading in the fading light, Kagiso finally flung open the door with Jonathan following behind. They walked up to Greeff, stopped in front of him, and Kagiso said, 'So, old man, how do we beat the alarm?' As he spoke, he produced a bottle of golden brown liquid from under his shirt. The old man's eyes were immediately drawn to the bottle as if it was his newborn child. Kagiso held it out to him, but pulled it back as Greeff reached out for it. 'Don't be greedy now, old man.'

'I've almost got it. You see… These sketches you gave me, they aren't very good,' Greeff said.

'They are all we have. You don't get nothing until you tell us what to do,' Kagiso warned, pulling up a chair.

For a while everyone watched Greeff as he sat bent over the sheets of paper. He coughed, deep and guttural, and wiped a slimy hand on his pants.

'He says it might not be possible to switch it off,' I said after a while, for no reason other than I was getting bored, and a little agitated that my evening read had been spoiled by their intrusion.

'Did you say that?' Kagiso said, looking at the old man.

'I might have. You never know, the way they make machines today anything is possible.'

'Don't fucking mess around, old man', Kagiso said.

Suddenly Kagiso grabbed one of the old man's ears. In the other he had a knife. 'You see this, old man?'

Greeff whimpered a quiet 'yes'.

'Now get your fucking act together or I'll cut you up,' Kagiso said, lightly pressing the blade against the man's neck. 'I stopped respecting my elders years ago.'

It was almost dark now, and the dinner bell would be ringing soon. We sat in silence while Greeff looked at the papers and scribbled things in the margins. 'I'd have to see the actual installation,' he said. 'These diagrams are all very generic. But if you want, I can try to explain.'

'Okay, old man, explain,' Kagiso said, once again taking the small bottle of brandy out and putting it on the table, his hand resting on it.

'Look at this,' Greeff said and pointed at one of the shapes on the page. 'This is the alarm switch. I don't think it will be visible. There is probably some electronics connected to it requiring a code. No biggie, if you open the box you should see something like this.' He pointed to a diagram. 'You want to cut that wire. Once that's done, you can switch off the current. There should be a marked switch for that, like this.'

He drew a squiggle-like shape.

'That simple?' Kagiso asked.

'Yes,' the old man said. 'That simple, providing you don't cut the wrong wire and set the alarms off.'

'And what about the cameras?' Jonathan asked.

'Cameras? Why you worried about the cameras? Simple, you switch off the lights at the back of the hospital. No light, and the cameras pick up nothing. Do I have to spell everything out for you?' He reached for the bottle as he spoke.

Kagiso let him have it.

We watched him twist the top, and lift the neck to his lips. He took a large swig. He coughed, splattering all over the papers.

'Jesus! Fuck, man! Do you have to be such a pig?' Kagiso

stood back. But the old man was already getting up. 'If you will excuse me, gentlemen, I need to get back to bed. I've had enough of this wild-goose chase.' He stumbled out of the room unsteadily, holding the bottle tightly under his shirt.

THERE ARE MANY DIFFERENT kinds of waiting. Some drive you crazier than others.

Sitting at my ward window, looking out at the dead, radiated world, I had been keeping myself busy these last years with the kind of waiting where you wait, but with no idea of how long. I knew death would eventually come, I could feel it weighing down my limbs at times, but for all its daily companionship it could have been two weeks away or two years. That kind of waiting I could make peace with.

That Monday morning, however, the world outside my window had a different look to it. It might have been as dead as always, but there lurked a promise of change out among the fence poles, out there where the dust snaps at your heels. Out there was some kind of freedom. What it would be like, I had little notion of. I knew, though, that it would not be the bright and promising future the others were imagining. Still, it lay out there like a large, undefined shape buried in the dry, red earth, waiting to be dug up.

A different shade of grey now hung over the horizon. Sitting there, I knew we would take our first stab at this new thing, this new way of living, in three days. I felt it edging nearer, like the rumble of the earth when there's a train in the distance. The clock was ticking, and for the first time in years the passing of time meant something to me. This kind of waiting was much more disconcerting.

I knew that my days of sitting by the window staring at the nothingness would soon be over. Even if we failed, nothing would ever be the same. In fact, things had already changed. But, until Thursday night came, I could imagine that I was still in that half-dead world I had occupied for the preceding three years, that twilight world with which I had long made peace. Not that I would have called what I felt nostalgia. After all, I would as soon see the hospital burn to the ground and say to hell with it... and so, too, to that man who lived there and answered to my name.

Still, three years is a long time. And even if there was nothing worth holding on to, the letting go still felt oddly unnatural. Something of the place was clinging to me the way molten tar clings to the soles of your shoes.

So I sat there looking out across the wires to the ridge, and then back down to where four cars stood parked over to the left. A soft breeze was covering them in a fine dust visible even from that distance. They would all need washing soon. I thought of what it must be like to sit in a car and to look through a dusty window like that, the sun catching the dirt particles, hiding the world in an orange blur. It stirred a memory from way back, but I let it go. I reminded myself that I was no longer interested in memories.

To the far left was the small, silver Hyundai. It occurred to me that I must have missed her, not noticed the car winding its way down the road that led down from the ridge. She must have pulled up, climbed out and walked across to the front entrance, all without me noticing a thing. Was my mind really that far away?

I thought that, as I sat there, she was in the hospital, probably placating some poor sod who couldn't keep his eyes off her. Then I thought that I probably wouldn't ever talk to her again, that she was one of the things I was leaving behind.

I lay down and slept, albeit fitfully. Even though I had been doing better since Von Hansmeyer's mysterious pill, I was still pretty out of it, and there was no way my wasting body was going to let me forget it. I slept long and dreamlessly.

When I got up many hours later the sun had shifted. I peered through the window, there were only three cars parked outside. 'Okay, now that's over too,' I said to my still-sleepy self.

So I made my way down the corridor to Von Hansmeyer's office. As I got closer, I could hear voices inside. I crept past and carefully pushed open the door of the room next door where I had spoken with Ms Van Vuuren. Nothing had changed. The same table and chairs. The walls as bare as ever. I was sure that I could detect the faintest remnants of her sweet perfume hanging in the air. I breathed in deeply, listening for that familiar silence. The surge of air made me dizzy, my head spin.

I stood for a moment wondering what the hell I was doing there. Then I told myself it was okay, that she was gone. I wasn't betraying myself. I wasn't slipping back into the world of wanting and needing. I was only saying goodbye. That's all.

From the window I could see the broken-down garden wall where I'd seen the man with the scar. There was no one down there now. Then I looked up at the fence and at the spot at the corner post where Jonathan had told me of the plans for escape. I was probably standing at the very window from which she and Von Hansmeyer had watched us.

I tried to imagine what the two of us would have looked like out there – Jonathan waving defiantly, me just standing there. Whichever way I pictured it, we made a sorry sight.

THOSE LAST FEW DAYS passed without much happening – at least, much that I was involved in. As I say, the logistics of escaping didn't really interest me. Ours was not to be a heroic Dirty Dozen job. After all, Pearson was no Alcatraz.

At some point, the guard clicked that after the escape he'd be left sitting in the security hub with a cut wire and a large 'Guilty' sign around his neck. He was on the point of pulling out of the whole thing altogether. Somehow, they made a deal. My guess is that Kagiso knew someone on the outside who was either threatening the guard and his family, or offering them a briefcase stuffed with cash.

The new plan was that there would be a decoy. Nothing major, just a noisy patient strolling out the front door. Our guard would go check what was up and some of the nurses or the guard at the gate would see him confronting the decoy, which would give him his alibi. As soon as he was out of the security hub, Kagiso was to slip in and cut the wire.

Kagiso and Sibu spent a lot of time that last week up in the old man's room at the dead-end of the hospital, talking about electronics and the like. I didn't know it then, but they were also grooming the old man to be their decoy. Knowing how much doubt he had about it all, they must have promised him more brandy than he could possibly drink in the little time he had left.

If the wire cutting worked, and there was no alarm and no current, the deal was that we would wait a while till things calmed down again. We figured no one would notice that the wires were dead. Then our guard would flick the switch for the security lights that lit up the back fence, and Kagiso and Sibu would run off in the dark to cut a hole.

As plans go, it didn't seem particularly well thought out to me, hardly foolproof. Still, given the general air of indifference that hung around the hospital, chances were that nothing more would be needed.

L ATE THURSDAY NIGHT. JONATHAN shook me by the shoulders. 'Come on, Barry,' he whispered impatiently. 'Get the fuck up. How can you be sleeping?' I was drowsy, but I got up. I dressed in the dark and before I could think any further he grabbed my arm and pulled me toward the door. 'There's a problem. Things have gone wrong,' he whispered. 'We don't have time.'

We crept barefoot down the corridor toward the stairs, shoes in hand, pillowcases with our meagre provisions slung over our shoulders. We paused and listened. Nothing. Then we tiptoed down to the landing. I stopped at the window from where I had once watched Kagiso and Espoir trying to fight each other to death, despite being too weak to do so.

The back yard was dark. It was the first time I had seen it that way since the new security systems were installed. So, the plan seems to be working, I thought. Maybe Jonathan was just putting on when he said that things had gone wrong.

When we got to the foot of the stairs, we stood back against the wall and waited. There was a light from the nurses' station in the front. Apart from the incessant whistle of the wind, there was no sound. Then, just as we were about to go, voices from out front. 'Lekker getik,' it came in thick Afrikaans. The sound of hard heels. Must be a guard. I held my breath. Thank God he didn't turn our way. But where was he going?

'Now,' Jonathan mouthed. I thought he was crazy, but I went nevertheless. We slipped across the wide downstairs passage and into the dining hall with its quiet rows of tables and chairs. Again I held my breath. Nothing. He hadn't seen or heard us.

Then, taking stock of what's around me, I saw it, and as a wave of nausea washed over me, I knew what had Jonathan so spooked. In a doorway that led from the dining hall to one of the back storerooms a dark shape like a pile of blankets lay motionless on the floor. There was a puddle and a smell of iron that I recognised as blood.

I couldn't help but stare. And suddenly I felt as if my own blood had stopped coursing through my veins, my pulse fading like the drums at the end of a tune on the radio. I was sure I was going to throw up.

But Jonathan half-shouted, half-whispered from his perch on the sill where he was about to climb out through an open window. So I turned away from the body on the floor. I noticed the breeze blowing in through the open window. I headed straight for it, hoisted myself up and, hesitating for just a nanosecond, leapt out into the darkness, my feet landing squarely in the long-abandoned flowerbed less than a metre below. Jonathan was waiting with five or six other men in the shadow of the building. We sat on our haunches against the wall, which still held some of the day's heat. We waited.

In the dark, about fifty metres off, we could just make out some movement. We strained our ears and listened, but it was quiet. Then, cutting through the stillness of the night, we heard a soft *click-click* as Kagiso and Sibu started to cut the wires.

We waited and it was quiet again. I was expecting an alarm at any moment, angry shouting, bright lights flashing in our faces. But nothing. Behind us, the hospital stood cold and heavy. Someone was coughing up in one of the wards and the coughing didn't stop. I couldn't help feeling guilty for everyone we were leaving behind.

'Let's go,' Jonathan whispered. 'They're through. No use waiting for the signal.'

He got up and, doubled over, led us across the yard to where Kagiso and Sibu had cut the hole. At least this was going according to plan. We squeezed through one by one.

As we waited for Morris and Adams to get through, I glanced back at the hospital, its dark shape silhouetted against the spotlights still beaming across the front entrance. I thought I heard someone laughing in the distance.

'Come on, don't get fucking nostalgic now,' Jonathan hissed and started off due north. I followed and so did Morris and Adams. The other men who had been with us were already gone.

Jonathan moved quickly with long, light strides. At first I kept up without a problem. It felt good to stretch my limbs. But after not even fifty metres my breath was already racing. For Jonathan it seemed effortless. I still have no idea how I managed to keep up with that dark figure ploughing on and on ahead of me.

After some minutes we came to a slight rise in the land. When we breached it, the earth fell away again in front of us and the dead flat plain stretched out into the distance, lit only by the Karoo moon.

Then, just a few steps down the slope, Jonathan stopped and slumped down to the ground. He was suddenly out of breath, wheezing with that strange mechanical whirr he made when sleeping. 'We're out of sight,' he coughed.

I collapsed next to him and, looking back, could see nothing but the rise we'd just crossed: the ridge that had demarcated our world for three years. There were no more lights, no hospital.

A half-moon floated a few inches above the horizon to the east as if it was a night like any other. The breeze was picking up now and far to the west was a thick bank of intense darkness. Clouds.

'I wonder if Kagiso and Sibu found their lift,' rasped Adams, who had managed to catch up, Morris in tow. No one answered. The four of us sat like that for a while, listening to each other struggling to inhale.

Then we heard the rhythmic thud of footsteps. Again I held my breath. It was approaching at a pace, closer and closer. And then, just as suddenly, passed only metres away. We hardly dared look, Jonathan's head in his hands, expecting the worst. When I lifted my head to peer into the blackness, just off to the west was a figure in white, little more than a shadow barely lighter than the ink-blotch night around him, was heading north. We saw him stumble, heard him curse, and then watched as he pulled himself up again and continued.

No one said anything.

We sat like that for a while, waiting for the ache in our lungs to subside. I took a swig of water and wondered why I hadn't brought more. All I had were the two one-litre plastic milk bottles, and how long would that last?

Then, over the soft swishing of the breeze, we heard the distant siren of the hospital alarm. It sounded closer than I thought it should. Any moment now they'll be on us, I thought. There was, after all, a dead man back there.

'Okay, we are heading northeast,' Jonathan whispered, looking up at the stars. He had traced this route for me on the map the previous day. 'First straight north to get away from the hospital and then northeast to shake off any pursuers.'

It wasn't the shortest route to a road or civilisation, but the shortest route would be too dangerous. Now, with the corpse, there was bound to be roadblocks too. Jonathan's plan was to keep going northeast until we hit the national road rather than the arterial road straight to the north. On the busy national road the odds of being picked up by the cops were much less, and we'd have a better chance of finding a ride. Only problem was that the map was rough and we didn't actually know how far it was to the national road or what terrain we would have to cross to get there.

With another quick glance up at the stars to confirm which way was northeast, he put his head down and started moving at a brisk pace. I followed a few paces after and behind me I heard Morris, still coughing, with Adams silently bringing up the rear. Far behind us I still heard the whining of the alarm, which seemed to be getting shriller and shriller.

The earth was hard underfoot. I stumbled over a thorny shrub. Ten metres later I stumbled over another one.

We were crossing one of those unnaturally flat stretches of Karoo. Ahead of us in the distance there lay, dimly outlined in the faint moonlight, a few small koppies. I thought that once we got there we'd be safe.

As we plodded on, I heard a man shouting far off in the distance. I don't know if any of the others heard it. If they did, they didn't show it. We just kept going. Whoever it was, fellow escapee or pursuer, we couldn't afford to be sidetracked.

Peaking back over my shoulder, far away I could now make out the lights of the hospital, a halo in a sea of darkness. For a moment I saw in front of me the scene in the dining hall, now with the long fluorescent lights on and cops taking fingerprints. I shook the thought from my head. Got to keep going, I thought. Focus on the dark koppies looming up ahead of us. Eyes on the prize.

To our left, the bank that had been building on the horizon had grown into a dark mass of cloud that was heading straight for us. Out there on that flat stretch of earth, looking at that approaching wall of moisture, I felt so damn alive. I knew that those clouds were blowing over from the west coast, that the cold front must have hit Cape Town earlier, and that it was drifting over a continuous mass of land to this moonscape in the Eastern Cape where I was edging my way. This was the real world. Not a silly dream.

We were out. We had escaped. For the first time in over three years, I was outside that cursed little square of land. I was back in the real world. Soon there would be cars and trucks and people going about their business.

But even as I felt all this, my lungs were burning. They were being torn apart. With each breath, their wounds gaped a little wider. I worried that my nodules would rupture again. There was no stopping, though.

I could hear Jonathan wheezing in front of me. Had I not known it was him, I might have been frightened of a dark figure like that, bent over, breathing like some bloodthirsty thing that wasn't quite human. And yet he just kept going, on and on and on. I don't know whether we would have had it in us to keep going if it wasn't for Jonathan out there leading the way.

'Lights! Jesus!' Adams blurted out from somewhere behind me, a bit too loudly for my liking. Far behind us a series of small lights was moving across the plain, pinpricks in the night. Then, over the gentle tugging of the breeze, I heard the distant barking of dogs.

'They have dogs,' I whispered. We stood listening, but no one else heard them.

'You sure?' said Jonathan. 'You're not imagining it?' There was a note of panic in his voice.

'Yes. Listen…' I said.

'Fuck,' Jonathan swore. He spat on the ground. We all heard it now. 'Keep up,' he muttered. We were going again, but faster now. It was still just a fast walk, but it was as much as our bodies could handle. As before, we moved in silence, but something felt different now. My heart beat adrenalin as it had when we first heard the alarm starting up.

Again the dogs barked in the distance, a wild, crazy barking, as if they smelled blood. I had no idea how far away they were. It crossed my mind that they must have caught someone, or maybe – maybe – they were on our trail, following our scent just metres behind. Perhaps they were already closing in and soon the flashlights would move in on us and the game would be up.

I didn't look back. In front of me, Jonathan didn't turn either. I knew then that if any of us dropped, he would leave us behind without a second thought. Earlier, he had gone back to get me in the ward, but I knew he wouldn't do that again.

Finally, after a long, tense trek across that veld, we reached the first of the koppies. Up close, it looked very different. It hunched there, set in the flatness around it like a massive tortoiseshell the size of a house. I looked back and could still see lights bobbing on the horizon behind us. There was no way of telling which direction they were heading.

Jonathan, though, didn't stop; he kept on walking – toward the second and then the third koppie. In all, there were probably about five of them clustered there. Finally, he stopped and looked around, and asked me what I thought. When I finally caught my breath enough to speak, I spluttered that I couldn't go any further.

'Neither can I, sport,' he said. 'Neither can I.'

Neither Morris nor Adams said a word; they couldn't. Both were equally buggered, it was clear. If we were to make a last stand, this would be the place.

We found a sheltered spot at the foot of the third koppie. We lay down on our backs in the sand, tucked between the small, hard shrubs. From our resting place, the view back toward the hospital was obscured by the first koppie we had passed. We could no longer see the lights of whatever authority was chasing us, and if we were still there by first light, they wouldn't see us either. It was about as safe as we could get right then. Which is not to say that the dogs wouldn't pick up our trail and lead them straight to us. But if we were lucky, they'd sniff out one of the other groups instead. It was a chance we had to take.

We lay there, listening to each other struggling to breathe. It was a peculiar jumble of wheezing, snorts and murmuring coughs. I couldn't help but laugh at the absurdity of it. When Morris asked what I was laughing at, I told him, and he also started laughing. Laughing and coughing.

And then, as our breathing slowly evened out, we just lay there, the sky turning above us, a million stars, just as it had always been. A million stars soon to be obscured by the oncoming clouds. Not that we were in the ideal condition to appreciate it, of course.

I heard Adams get up and watched as he moved off to go vomit somewhere where we wouldn't have to endure it. His body wasn't handling the escape very well at all. Truth be told, I wasn't feeling too great myself. As so many times before in the ward, I felt my limbs grow leaden, as if death itself was weighing them down. This time, though, it was accompanied by a fire in my lungs that just wouldn't go out, flames that reached up my throat like an eager vine of acid intent on smothering me. Instead of blowing fire, though, I coughed pathetic smatterings of blood.

Still, looking back, maybe that was, after all, the ideal time to witness a perfect sky like that. For all our aches and pains, we were newly freed men. We had been given a reprieve, and maybe more so than for anyone else, being out there under that firmament meant something to us – as if there was a message hidden in it all, a message written up there just for us.

I heard the familiar wheeze of Jonathan's snoring. Out in the open, it sounded different, somehow less menacing than before. To the other side of me, Morris was lying very still. He must have been asleep too. I hoisted myself up onto my elbows and noticed Adams sitting cross-legged some thirty metres off and it occurred to me that I didn't really have any idea who he was.

I lay back down again and watched as the clouds moved slowly across the canopy above us, obscuring the stars. The breeze was much stronger now and I knew that it wouldn't be long before we felt the large, warm drops of a Karoo rainstorm. We would have nowhere to hide. But even that didn't matter.

And then I was out like a rock.

I came to in the pail flush of morning with Jonathan standing over me.

'Come on, sport,' he said. 'We got to get going.'

I shivered. Following the rain, the soft damp of the earth had seeped up into my bones, and I felt the clammy clinging of my clothes on my skin. I sat up. Toward the east, the first grey stain of daylight was already discolouring the last remaining clouds and the irregular strips of sky between them. Almost four o'clock, I thought.

We'd been lucky. We had made it through the night. The dogs hadn't managed to sniff out our sleeping bodies. And with the rain that fell during the night, there was a good chance that our tracks were washed away, the last wire that connected us to that place. Cut. Leaving us free to drift off. Maybe luck was on our side, after all.

I reached into the pillowcase I was using as a bag. I pulled out a slice of brown bread I had stolen from the previous evening's dinner table. It had gotten wet in the night. I ate it slowly. My throat felt thick and swollen. Even though the bread was moist, I could hardly get it down without water.

Jonathan was quietly talking to Adams, who was still slumped in precisely the same spot where he had been before I fell asleep. Jonathan held out a hand, but Adams didn't move. Then Jonathan said something else and Adams relented, letting himself be hoisted to his feet.

'Okay, we're off,' Jonathan said as he came toward me, and once again we were on our way.

We emerged from the cluster of koppies onto another large, flat plain stretching as far as the eye can see. There weren't any further koppies in sight.

'We'd better move quickly,' Jonathan said. 'There's no place for us to hide once the sun comes up.'

The smell of rain still lingered in the air, but the last clouds were already drifting off. It couldn't have rained much.

Beneath the softly discoloured surface, the earth was still as hard and seemed no less dry than before. In that chilly pre-dawn there lingered something pure and mystical, like a mist that had drifted in from another world. Something you wanted to suck deep into your lungs and hang on to for later.

As we walked, light slowly began to flood the eastern sky, and too soon the first bright shards of yellow sunlight flashed over the horizon. After maybe two hours on foot, we stopped and drank. We had been going northeast all the while. In the direction from where we had come, we could see the koppies, sticking out of the plain like the half-buried eggs of some giant bird. There was no sign of anyone following us.

I stood scanning the horizon around us. Then I saw a blip on the skyline to the east. I was looking straight into the sun, so it was hard to tell, but there did seem to be a short vertical line, a line where sky met land, that seemed just too straight to be the random creation of nature.

'What do you think that is?' I said and pointed it out to Jonathan.

He stood looking, his hand over his eyes. 'A building?' he asked. 'Don't know. Doesn't look like a building, but doesn't look natural either. May be just a wall?'

'I think we should check it out. There might be people there, but what the heck… We'll just have to be careful.'

'It wouldn't take us closer to the road,' I pointed out. Our progress on the map would be bending into a line running parallel to the national road to the north.

'I know,' Jonathan said with a hint of impatience, 'but we're going to need shelter soon. I don't want to die out here in this godforsaken place.'

And that was that. We adjusted our course from northeast to east and headed for that point just to the left of the rising sun. Whatever it was we were moving toward, it remained a kink on the horizon for a very long time. Whether it was very far or whether we were just moving very slowly, I couldn't tell.

Then it was mid-morning and the sun was high and

merciless, beating down on us with a nuclear hatred so intense I could feel my skin turning papery under its glare. Whatever moisture there'd been earlier in the day had, by then, been sucked from the earth. Again I felt my limbs getting heavier and heavier. I felt my mind narrow. Whereas earlier in the day I could string together clear thoughts, all I could manage now was to focus on Jonathan's form in front of me and to urge my body to keep going. For all the openness around me, I had descended into a burning hot tunnel.

I was right there in that impersonal burial yard of the gods I had looked upon so many times from my ward window. But whereas that image had had a fence, a ridge and a road, the one I faced now had nothing. It was just hard, indifferent nothingness.

I heard gunshots in the distance. I glanced at the others, but again no one else seemed to have noticed. Was I imagining things? They wouldn't really be hunting the escapees down like dogs, would they? They wouldn't have to. No point in mentioning it to the others then, I thought.

Trudging on was all I could do, all anyone could do. As I walked, I sucked the last drops of water from my first water bottle and dropped it in the veld. We hadn't even been gone twelve hours, and already my supplies had been halved. I was on the verge of collapse.

With every step further away from the hospital, I felt the fatigue getting worse. It crossed my mind that we might have sinned against some god of this land, that by crawling through that fence we had brought shame upon ourselves. We'd be cursed to wander about and die out in the wilderness. We had committed a mortal sin when we let ourselves be led by a man like Jonathan Fox.

By midday it had become clear that what we had seen on the distant horizon was the remains of a building. We couldn't yet make out much more than that, but there was certainly no sign of life, no colour, no human activity. Jonathan put his hand up when we were about half a kilometre away. We stood and watched for a while. The land here rose and fell softly like large, flat waves. The wall ahead of us was the only straight line in a world of contours. There was no smoke, no colour, no movement.

'Okay then... Let's take a look,' Jonathan said, and waved us forward. About a hundred metres from the ruins, we stumbled across an old dirt road. It was little more than some lines of eroded topsoil and an absence of Karoo shrubs that happened to take the shape of a road, but there it was. It led straight toward the decaying walls. In the other direction, to our left, the path disappeared between two low swells, no doubt on its way to the national road to the north.

The kink we had seen on the horizon was one side of the dilapidated remains of a very old building. It had no roof, just holes where windows had once been, a set of walls, some crumbling away, shaped into two large rooms, empty inside but for bits of rubble and a hard clay floor with cracks like crow's feet.

The four of us collapsed in a thin strip of shade against one of the inside walls. I closed my eyes and wished for the wind to blow. There would be no more wind, though. From years of looking out of the ward window I knew that the rain of the previous night was already more than what we could ever have asked for. If there was to be any mercy, that had been it.

I reached for my remaining water bottle. Lightly I let the water soothe my parched lips and mouth. I knew that I should keep it for later, but I couldn't help myself. It felt sweeter than the sweetest sin. I wanted to throw my head back and take large gulps and then let the remainder run out over my face.

But I didn't. When I looked up at the bleached blue-white sky, I felt my balance begin to falter, so I closed my eyes and shut out the world. But even with my eyes closed, it was as if my retinas had sucked up the day's glare and were now radiating it back into my eyeballs. My whole body felt like that, a dried-up sponge saturated with sunlight. Had the world suddenly went dark I would have glowed like a firefly.

I don't know if I actually slept. It could be that I just slipped out into that half-woken sunstroke world where clocks slow down and speed up with no predictability whatsoever. I remember noticing later, though, that Morris and Adams were no longer with us in that strip of shade. The shadow along the wall had shifted, the day still mercilessly hot, but they were gone.

'Where are they? Morris and Adams,' I asked Jonathan. He was crouched a few steps away, his eyes open, his head propped against the wall behind him. With his uncombed hair and drawn face, he looked more ragged than I had ever seen him. Maybe we could pass ourselves off as bums when we reached the city, I thought.

'Adams was going to be sick again. Morris went to look for him,' Jonathan said, his voice dry and rough.

'How long ago?'

'Can't rightly say, sport.'

We sat in silence for a while, hoping that the faintest of breezes would turn into something more. I felt myself drifting off again.

'Who was the guy in the kitchen?' I asked Jonathan after what could have been two minutes as easily as it could have been an hour. For some inexplicable reason my mind had once again conjured that image of the lit-up doorway, the once-human pile in a pool of blood.

He looked at me, his head at a slight angle. 'Dugan.'

'Dugan? Tall guy, used to hand out the meds?'

'Yup.'

And then it fell into place. The shape on the floor could only have been him. The broad shoulders, the sheer size of him, the man who danced with Ms Van Vuuren in my dreams, who had held her and drawn her yielding body into a corner.

'I think he must've heard someone messing about in the

pharmacy storeroom where they keep the pills,' Jonathan said, his voice slow and deliberate. 'He went looking and got hit on the back of the head. The way I see it, he didn't know Kagiso was hanging back on the outside. So, as he is standing with his hand on the door handle, about to go in, Kagiso steps out of the shadows and takes a shot. And that's that.'

'And that's that.'

'Well, after that, Sibu came out with a garbage bag full of pills. Kinda explains it, doesn't it?'

We sat for a while. There was still no breeze. 'Is it really us and them like that?' I said.

Jonathan thought for a moment. 'No,' he said. I waited for him to say more, but he didn't.

By late afternoon, the other two weren't back yet. I pulled myself up onto my feet with great effort, my limbs having grown stiff in the hours I'd sat dozing. I stumbled back out to the road and scanned the dusty path for footsteps. I didn't find any.

'They went that way,' Jonathan said behind me. He pointed to where the remains of the path disappeared between two slight rises.

'Okay, let's go then.'

The sun threw long shadows as we walked. The breeze was finally picking up; it wasn't cool, or even very strong, but it did just enough to take the edge off the heat.

The road eventually passed between two low hills and then veered off to the right to avoid another, steeper hill. As we walked, we saw faint footprints here and there. Some stretched out like long, sad skid marks as Adams's legs must have lost what strength remained in them.

Trudging our way down the slight incline, following the others' faint tracks, Jonathan suddenly put his arm out. He stood dead still. I followed his eyes off to the left, to a spot beyond where the hill dropped away. Then I saw it. Grey, almost indistinguishable from its surroundings, the clear straight lines of a zinc roof. Even from that distance, it didn't look old.

'We have company,' Jonathan whispered under his breath.

I glanced back down at the ground. The two trails of footprints were still there, heading straight ahead, lingering in the dust. Either they hadn't seen the house or they didn't care. Ahead of us there was no sign of them.

'I think we'd better wait it out,' Jonathan said. 'We don't want to get spotted out here. We can take a closer look when it's dark.'

He had a point, so we tracked back to a spot where the hill shielded us from the house. We lay down flat on our backs and waited. It was all we could do to hide.

The sky was as empty as if it had never contained a thing. The thought of clouds up there seemed impossible. It was just a vast, pale nothingness. Despite my sorry state, I found this pale emptiness quite reassuring. Yes, some barely audible voice seemed to tell me there was nothing out there. No need to worry. There is no great mystery that needs unfolding.

But at the same time I knew that the night would come and we would go looking for the other two and that we might not find them; or that someone else might already have found them.

As it was, I didn't have to wait for nightfall to have my illusion of peace shattered. As we lay there staring at the sky, we heard shouting from the direction of the house. A single gunshot rang out over the hard, dead earth. It sounded terribly close. I felt my tired muscles tense up. Then it was quiet again. I looked at Jonathan to see what he was thinking. He looked back at me, but his eyes were large and dull, as if he had no flight response left in his body.

'Maybe we should run,' I whispered.

He shook his head.

So we just lay there, holding our breaths, waiting it out. I kept my eyes on the line where sky met horizon, expecting men in police or army uniforms to appear any moment and aim their gleaming weapons on us. No one came, and neither did I hear any more shouting or gunshots.

Next to me, Jonathan was breathing harder and heavier. He turned onto his side and started coughing, convulsions shaking his whole body. He reminded me of a boy as he lay there. Whatever confidence he had once exuded had been stripped away. I'm ashamed to say it, but his childlike body revolted me. It seemed sick that such boyish limbs should be attached to a man. How could such a wasted body succeed in the serious business of escaping from a quarantine hospital?

His coughing stopped and he lay still. I wondered if he was still alive. 'You okay?' I asked.

He grunted in a way that I took to mean yes.

I knew, though, that he was not well. Earlier that afternoon his eyes had had a dullness about them I had never seen before. He no longer had the forceful push ahead he'd had the previous night on the plain. When he walked, it was as if he wasn't really walking, but just directing the little momentum he had left.

Dusk came. When it was almost dark, I sat up. Off to the west, the sky still glowed red, but to the east it was already a dark, dirty colour.

'I think it's late enough,' I said. 'Lets get going.'

Jonathan turned his head to look at me, but it was as if he was looking right through me.

'Come on,' I said.

'Sure, sport,' he said and slowly pressed himself up on his feet. Rather than follow the rough road, we cut across to the left and climbed the low slope of the hill that stood there. When we reached the top, we crouched down on our haunches. We'd stand out like gothic pillars against the skyline if anyone down at the house took the time to look up.

Below us, the landscape was dark, almost too dark to make out any detail. The house was clear enough though, a large much darker patch against the red earth. From a window, a pale yellow light cast long rectangles onto the earth outside.

I listened, but could hear nothing.

As my eyes grew accustomed to the light, I made out an outbuilding, likely a garage, to the left of the house. The light from the window fell on a strip of concrete to the side of it. We sat watching for a while.

'Shall we take a closer look?' I asked. Jonathan didn't answer. 'You think they're there?'

'No,' he said. 'And if they are, there is nothing we can do about it.' 'Where else would they be? Those tracks lead to the house, I'm sure of that.'

'Maybe they're camped out somewhere on the other side,' he said. 'Just like we are here.'

'But what we heard... Something happened. Maybe they're locked up down there. Or maybe they've already been caught, been hauled back to the hospital.'

I froze. Down below, a door had opened and the silhouette of a man stood etched against the pool of light spilling out. He held out a hand and then tossed something into the darkness with a flick of the wrist. Only then did I see the large black dog.

The man lit up a pipe and stood there in the filtered light smoking for a long time, peering out somewhere to the north of the hill we were on.

In front of him, the dog sat waiting patiently for more of what he had been tossed.

Eventually the man put out his pipe and stepped back inside, closing the door behind him and leaving the dog outside.

'We're not going down there,' Jonathan said.

We tracked back down the hill and continued in the direction in which the other two had gone. It was dark now and the moon had grown thinner since the previous night. We could no longer make out any footprints, but we knew well enough that they too would have kept to the outline of what remained of the path ahead.

Before too long, the route started curving to the left. As

Jonathan had predicted, it was turning toward the house. We decided to follow it until we could see the building. Surely that was as far as the other two would have gone. Even that was too far, stupid even. Adams could barely walk. It was hard to believe that he had even come this far.

I peered into the dark, expecting the dog to charge us at any moment. There would be no hope for us. There would be no way for us to fight off an animal like that.

Then I picked up the sickening sour-milk tang of vomit and I knew we were close. I whispered to Jonathan to stop, but he had also smelt it and was already trying to figure out where it came from. We found it next to the road, covered up with loose sand. There was no sign of either Adams or Morris.

I stepped in something, a viscous substance underfoot that nearly made me lose my footing on the hardened ground, and when I bent down I could tell right away that it was blood. Had our poor comrade coughed it or bled it?

Far ahead, the faint light stilled flickered through the window of the house. Too much noise and the dog would come running. If Adams was vomiting out here in the middle of the day, someone would have noticed.

'Maybe he's got them locked up in his garage,' I whispered.

'Hell knows, sport,' Jonathan shrugged and, after a long pause looking toward the hazy light from that man's window, he turned around and started walking.

So we had turned back once again. I suppose it was all we could do, Giving up on the other two didn't feel right. But there was nothing to be done, no point. There was the gunshot, the voices, the shouting... there was certainly more than one man there that afternoon, and that meant someone had come. It was now just the two of us.

'Let's try for the highway tomorrow,' Jonathan said when we had tracked back some way down the dirt path. I felt we should keep going east and then turn north again once we'd put some distance between the house and us. But Jonathan said he couldn't. He wanted to go back to the old ruin where we had spent the afternoon. The way he said it made it clear that he wasn't up to negotiating. 'Do what you want, sport. I'm going back.'

After what felt like many hours we reached the spooky outlines of the old house. In the dark it looked as though there would be ghosts drifting about inside.

'Let us then be the ghosts to haunt this long-dead place. Let us strike fear into the hearts of those who gaze upon us… fear and disgust in equal measure.'

This is what I wanted to write in my notebook as I lay on that hard floor, letting my fingers play over its cracked surface. I should have brought a notebook along, I thought. I was like a child who had left his favourite toy at home.

But, no, I wasn't like a child at all. As I lay there I felt as old as no man of thirty-two should ever feel. I felt myself dying, just as I knew the man who lay against the opposite wall was also dying. How appropriate that we would return to this place, where we could be old with those skeletal ruins, where we could lament our lost lives as it laments the loss of the life and voices that once echoed between its walls.

Above the spot where I lay, a thick nail stuck out of the wall at an odd angle. I reached up and ran my fingers over its rusty surface. Some long-dead man had put that there and hadn't thought on it twice. He had hammered it in there in a time when he still had hope for the building and its purpose; when the house was worth building, or at least still worth saving.

Apart from the nail, that man had left no sign. No strip of tough, coarse fabric, no broken pots or pans, no door handles or legs of chairs, nothing from which to reconstruct a possible past. It was just a set of crumbling walls and a clay floor out in the middle of nowhere. And now it had two ghosts.

I wanted to thank that man for leaving his house for us and for leaving it so bare. How kind of him to have stripped it clear in preparation for our coming, to be away and not to bother us with tea and small talk. How kind to let me lie on that bare floor and look upon the stars and the deep dark blue that held them; to let me rest there as if it were my own kitchen. How kind of him to have left this world to make room for us.

Then I fell asleep and dreamt that I was back in the ward, seated at my usual place in front of the window.

A thin layer of snow covered the cold, red earth. Slivers of white clung to the wire fencing like spiderwebs stretched to breaking. The fence posts stood cold and metallic in the crisp air. The vague pattern of a car's tracks could be made out on the whitened road that led up to the ridge.

Below the window was a ragtag of cars and old-fashioned horse-drawn carriages, all black with gold trimmings. As before, they had drawn up in a large circle. The front of the hospital didn't look like that in real life, I thought. But what could I do, there it was.

I felt the urge to sketch the unusual view from my window, so I reached for my drawer and slid it open. The notebooks weren't there. I got up and rummaged through all the drawers, and then the bedclothes, under the mattress. They were gone.

I had been alone in the ward until then, but as I was looking for the notebooks, I sensed that someone was watching me. When I looked up, the man with the scarred face was standing in the doorway, leaning against its frame, arms folded, an expression on his face that looked like faked pity.

'I'm looking for my notebooks,' I said. 'You don't perhaps know who might have taken them?'

'What notebooks?' he said, and smiled.

'Never mind.'

Only then did I notice that he was dressed up, smart in a suit and tie.

It didn't quite fit him. Something seemed to jar, as if the sleeves were too long and the shoulders just a little too narrow.

'Why are you wearing a suit?' I asked him.

'The ball, of course,' he said. 'Surely you saw all the guests arriving when you were sitting there staring out of the window in that serious manner of yours.'

Even though it sounded like English and I could understand him, my dream self believed he was speaking Polish. I still don't know why that is. He had spoken Polish in a previous dream as well. But surely the real man, the man I had seen that day sitting on the wall while I was waiting for Ms Van Vuuren, wouldn't have been Polish.

'Are you coming down?' he asked. 'Maybe there is someone who wants to see you.'

'Who?'

'Come on, get dressed. I can't wait all day.'

When I looked in my cupboard, all I found was the same old navy-blue suit I had last worn in high school. This time, however, I could hardly squeeze into it. The jacket had only one button now and I felt the sleeve tearing where it met the shoulder. Compared to me, the man with the scar was dressed to kill.

I wanted to splash some water on my face and run a comb through my hair, but he scowled. So I let it be and walked ahead of him out into the corridor and down the stairs. At the foot of the stairs my instinct told me to turn left, to follow the sound of violins and chatter blowing over from the ballroom like a warm breath. I even imagined I could smell the waxy odour of resin beneath the perfume that hung where guests must have passed moments before.

'No, right! We're going right,' the man with the scar instructed.

Whereas his tone had been mocking earlier, taunting even, he now sounded angry.

So I turned right. The hallway was deserted. No yellow light beckoned.

I didn't know where I was going, yet it was as if something was leading me. I turned into the dining hall and saw a group of people gathered around a table on the furthest side. Ms Van Vuuren, in a white evening gown, Dugan in a neat black tuxedo, and four or five other men I didn't know.

As I approached, they all burst out laughing at something she was reading to them. She instinctively hid her face behind her hand as she giggled, but the men folded double and slapped each other on the shoulders. Their flushed faces had almost pained expressions.

Then, when I was just a few steps from the table, a tall, thin man noticed me and suddenly went quiet. He nudged his friend, who, on seeing me, did the same. Then I saw that the book Ms Van Vuuren had been reading from was one of my notebooks. Three more of the notebooks lay scattered across the table. One man had put a beer glass down on one of them.

By then she had also seen me. I watched as her expression changed from a smile to horror. Except for one man who still snorted helplessly, they were all quiet. She stood up and, coming toward me, said, 'I'm sorry, Barry. You shouldn't take it personally.' She reached out to touch my arm with her white-gloved hand. But she stopped short, as if she remembered my sickness just in time.

I wanted to say something, but nothing came out.

Dugan stepped forward and, placing his palm in the small of her back, whispered something in her ear. She looked up at him and blushed.

'No harm done,' he boomed. 'Come on, everyone, they'll be waiting for us in the ballroom.' She hooked into his arm and they led the way out, the others following.

I walked over to the table where the notebooks lay discarded. One already had a ring on it from the beer glass, some of its pages drenched in stale, watery beer. Another book had pages torn out, another lists of phone numbers scrawled on the cover.

'What did you expect?' the man with the scar said behind me in his Slavic drawl. 'You were away so long. We thought you'd never come back.'

I didn't answer. Instead I just gathered up the books and turned to leave.

By then, he had moved over to the door that led from the dining hall to the storeroom that served as a dispensary, where they kept the meds.

'Was it like this?' he asked, and went down on his knees. Then he lay down on the floor, supporting his head on his arm.

But I have just seen Dugan, I thought.

'Or was it like this?' he said, and stretched out one arm, twisting his head to the left in an unnatural pose.

I left him lying there and walked out, back up in the direction of the ward. I remember thinking that I should get out of the place. I wondered if Jonathan's plans were still on course. Maybe he'd be in the ward and I could ask him. Maybe he'd have some idea of what was going on.

Halfway up the stairs I stopped. I stood listening to the muffled strains of the orchestra drifting through the corridors like a thick mist. The music strangely alluring, as if the Balkan horn was about to open a portal to another world – and that the cost of entry to this world would be paid in absurdity. I could hear the voices of people singing along, ever more boisterous and intoxicated.

When I awoke, it was on a cold clay floor with the stars above me.

Jonathan, lying against the wall opposite me, wasn't snoring that strange otherworldly snore of his that I had come to know so well. I watched him, my eyes still thick with sleep and Ms Van Vuuren's presence still lingering just a moment away.

Then I realised that he wasn't moving. He lay with his mouth open, no sign of movement in either his nostrils or his throat. His face was distorted like a mask from some ghoulish puppet show, teeth and gums exposed, eyes staring blindly. The sleeve had shifted up his right arm as he had slept. Already the arm had a blue stain spreading underneath the soft white skin.

Far above, the last stars were barely visible in the pre-dawn light. The day would break soon and I would have to deal with the dead man lying with me. And, who knows, the day might also be my last.

My skin tingled with the coolness of the morning air. I lay paralysed at the prospect of the day ahead of me. Finally, when it was lighter, I sat up and drank the last of my water. I wanted to toast Jonathan or pay homage to him in some other way, but I didn't. Instead I just stared out through the space where a door had once been, at the red earth and throwaway plants that stretched and then disappeared into the distant light of the morning.

Then I got up and walked around, kicking at the ground. At the side furthest from the road I found what I was looking for. That someone had once tried to plant something there seemed unthinkable, but someone had. Not that there were signs of any plant life beyond the normal Karoo scrub. Whatever basil or onions or rosemary had once grown on that square patch of earth was long gone. I dug the heel of my shoe into the soil and after a few stomps the surface broke. Underneath the harder crust it was sandy and soft.

I walked back to where Jonathan lay and slid his bag out from where he had propped it between himself and the wall. The knife wasn't there. I found it in the left pocket of his pants, a steak knife, still dirty, stained with a dark red goo, probably stolen from the hospital kitchen. I sat down and started hacking at my empty water bottle. After a minute the bottom half came loose. I coaxed the last few drops from it and went back to the garden where I started shovelling out sand with my makeshift trowel.

The going was slow. As I shovelled, the soft sand beneath the hardened topsoil kept running back into the hole. Maybe I should have thought of something better, but I couldn't.

To the east the sun was rising, and before long the sweat was once again streaming down my temples, down my neck and back. My arm was tired and I felt like giving up. I thought of leaving Jonathan in the house. But, no, who does such a thing? So I kept digging.

The sun was already hovering a good few degrees above the horizon when I finally had something approaching a shallow grave. Roughly what I thought was Jonathan's size, about thirty to forty centimetres deep. It would have to do.

I went round to the front of the house. Odd thing was that, as I was about to enter through the gaping whole in the brickwork, I suddenly felt the need to knock on a door. It was as if some reverse magnetism was urging me away from there and telling me not to enter. I should be wearing a suit and tie, I thought.

So I hung back for a minute out front, listening to the silence and smelling the dust on the air. I looked at the remains of the old dirt road that disappeared between the two low hills. Over there, over there are people; there are churches and cemeteries where proper burials can be held. Over there, there are funeral regulations and families of mourners to consider, letters to be sent and calls to be made.

I didn't even know whether he had any family.

Then, despite how wrong it felt, I turned around and went in. I picked Jonathan's rigid body up under the shoulders and dragged him out the door and round the house, his feet carving snake lines in the sand. Even to my weakened arms his body felt strangely light. In death his body's transformation back into that of a child was complete.

I laid him down in the hole with what gentleness I could muster. He barely fit. I had to twist his stiff legs and fold his arms tight over his stomach. I propped his head to the side so that his mouth would stay closed. Then I pulled his eyelids down with my thumbs and sat looking at him.

'What the fuck did you have to go do that for?'

As if to respond, his limp head shifted a centimetre to the left as his body settled in the sand.

Then I started covering him up, not with the careful digging of before, but shovelling the loose earth over him with my hands. I had to get it over with. What had been bearable before had turned into a nightmare.

I felt an animal moan in my chest. I beat my fist against the old back wall until it cracked and the side of my hand was raw. I felt my mind going. 'What kind of a God allows this?'

When I eventually managed to cover most of him, I looked down at the mound. Anyone peeking around the back of the house would see that something was buried there. Maybe the dog we saw back at the house would dig him up, I thought. Maybe one day the dog would pad up to his master with Jonathan's arm in his mouth and soon after the police would be out here digging up the rest of him. And maybe then they'd come looking for me.

I went back inside the ruin. The inside wall was only one brick in width. I stood back against the far wall and, with a three-step run-up, threw all my weight behind my shoulder and rammed into it. To my surprise it gave. A large strip next to the inner doorway broke off and crumbled, scattering chunks of brick and mortar across the ground as it fell.

I picked up the largest of the pieces, the size of a chessboard, and carried it round back, laying it down over the place where Jonathan's head lay. Then I took out the knife and etched in large letters on the slab just one word: 'Jonathan.' And then, with no idea what else to write, I carved out the words, 'Rest in peace.'

I would have liked to have left then, but the exertion had drained me and when I tasted my own blood and wiped my mouth, the back of my hand was stained red. So I lay down in a strip of shade inside the ruined house and rested. To my surprise, I had discovered a bottle still half-filled with water in Jonathan's bag. He had clearly been holding out on me and, truth be told, I hadn't taken much notice of whether he drank or not, or even considered offering him any of mine. Naturally, I drank from it, ignoring the threat of cross infection that shot through my mind like an institutional directive. What if I got infected by a second strain? Surely it didn't matter at this point?

I lay there wondering if I, too, was going to die there. But something in the air told me I wasn't. For all the lead in my limbs, there was still some force that urged me to keep going. Then I thought how odd it was that I was the only one left out here. Me, the one who was only tagging along, the one who knew from the outset that there would be nothing out here. Nothing to run to, nothing to find.

I lay amongst the ruins all that afternoon. I must have dozed off again, and had it not been for a horrible coughing fit, I might have slept all day. When I woke, it was from a disjointed sleep and to find myself drenched in sweat. The sun had shifted and I was fully exposed to that deathly radiation, so I moved to a shady strip of ground against another wall and drifted off again.

When I woke next, it was dusk and I was running a fever. I toyed with the idea of staying there, waiting for the reaper to come and drag me off, but as dusk turned to darkness, I pulled myself together. My limbs felt like dead weights and even just standing made me feel as if all my muscles were stretched to the point of breaking, tearing from the bone. But, as I say, there was some strange force pulling me on.

I struggled to my feet and set out along the skeleton of a road we had taken before and just kept going due east, where the road turned off toward the house. My plan was simple – put some distance between me and the house and then turn north to the national road.

Once again the land lay like large, flat waves in the dim moonlight. I felt the last of the day's heat radiating from the earth and then just hang there in the stagnant night air. Conditions meant that I made good ground though. Travelling on my own, there was no one else to consider, and no one else considering me. I was alone, and my outlook on the world around me changed as it does when one is alone. Every shadow, every stick in the sand, everything seemed just a little sharper. I had to be on the lookout now. There was no Jonathan to caution with the lift of an arm.

Around me, the veld was as lifeless as before, and yet it seemed as if life was just another step further. At any instant a snake could slither out of a hole in front of me, or some last, desperate search party would appear in the distance and I'll hear the far-off barking of dogs.

But I told myself it was safe. I was already about an hour's walk east of the house. Despite the fatigue in my legs, I managed to climb a small rise – it could hardly be called a hill – but I nevertheless felt the difference between even the feeble incline and the flat walk I had had up until then.

At the top, I sat down. Far to the north, a small light moved across the plain, and then another from the opposite direction. The highway. Even in the stillness, with no wind, I could hear nothing. I guessed it to be about four or five kilometres away. It was hard to gauge.

It occurred to me that the last time I had looked upon a distant road like that was through a window. And then another memory, another window, another time and place drifted back. I was about ten years old, on holiday with my mother and some of her family. I couldn't sleep and lay staring out of a bedroom window at the distant back and forth of that single strip of lights, forever caught up in that one line, never to move beyond it.

I spat in the dirt. What use are memories when what lies between you and them is a wasteland? What good are the pictures of lost loved ones if you no longer have the eyes to see them? It is as God told Lot... looking back is madness.

Back in the direction from which I'd come, I imagined I could see a very faint light, but I wasn't sure. I thought of the man who had stood in that doorway smoking his pipe. Maybe he, too, carried the bug. Maybe that was why he was living out here, self-preservation in isolation, self-imposed exile. He certainly wasn't farming or using the land in any other way. Clearly he didn't want to be among people. Maybe I would have liked to have met that man.

Suddenly I felt the hair on the back of my neck stand upright. Something had moved in the dark. It couldn't have been more than a hundred metres away, down at the bottom of the hill in the direction from which I had come. Then I saw it again, a large, dark shape, shifting indefinably against a dark background. It made no sound, just a shadow without form, and yet I interpreted its very presence as menacing, foreboding. Was this how death would come for me?

Slowly, trying to be as quiet as possible, I scrambled up and across the summit and, huddled over, shuffled down the other side, off toward the north so as to put the hill between me and whatever it was lurking in the shadows. It might have been another escapee, in which case I probably had no reason to be scared, but then it could just as easily have been the man we had seen, or a wild animal, or who knows what.

I heard a rustling behind me. It was coming closer. I started running, or at least the closest thing to a run that my broken body was capable of. There was something chasing me, I was sure now. I didn't dare look back.

I ran as fast as I could. Then, quite suddenly, there was nothing under me and for a long moment I was flying. I crashed down, hitting the hard earth with a force that shuddered through my bones... I felt the skin scraping off my left knee and my hands stinging with the impact. I tried to pull myself up but a lightning bolt of pain shot through my leg.

Whatever it was that was chasing me was getting closer and closer, I could sense it closing in.

And then I didn't care any more. I lay on my side and, instead of trying to run or fishing out Jonathan's steak knife for a fight, I closed my eyes and waited. Whatever it was, let it take me. Whatever it was, surely I had seen worse, surely I had nothing more to fear. What useless thing inside me had run in the first place? If there was a demon to meet out here, surely I should face it head on. If it was Jonathan come to haunt me, I should be glad, grateful even. Either way, it dawned on me that there would be no more running, and that thought comforted me.

When I opened my eyes, the black shape was standing on the outcrop above me, etched out above the half-metre drop. Gracefully, it slipped down and came toward me. The demon had taken the shape of a large four-legged animal. It walked up to me and licked my face with a long, sloppy-wet tongue.

It sniffed my neck. With its warm, gushing breath at my jugular, I wished for it to open its jaw and to sink its fangs into my sinewy flesh. At that moment, I would not have minded. As I say, I had found a peace just then that I hadn't felt before. And had it sunk its canines into my neck like a vampire, I would have stroked its head with all the tenderness I had left and begged it to sit by me while the stars faded above.

'We will sacrifice ourselves to those who dare not have us.'

The dog sniffed the ground and then, retreating a few steps, circled twice and lay down. It watched me intently.

I tried to get up. I felt the wetness against my pants where my left knee was bleeding, but there was something else wrong… inside. Once again pain shot through my bones like an electrical current.

Eventually I struggled up. As long as I kept the leg straight I'd be okay, I thought.

I looked over at the dog and it, too, got to its feet. I held my hand out and it came closer. He let me scratch his ear as if it was the most natural thing in the world. Oh, how I had missed dogs these last three years. I had completely forgotten that such good and gentle creatures exist in the world. Then he pulled away and traced something with his nose on the ground. He scratched at the earth with his paw, and I bent over to see. There was a hole in the ground. Snake, I thought.

The dog sat, looking first at the hole and then at me. I turned and, with my bad leg, started hobbling northward. The large, black shape came with me, all the time exploring the veld around us, finding things in the dirt to stick his nose into, things I never knew were there.

But after a while, when I looked around he was gone.

The going was slow that night. Still, after a few hours in a dream-like march, I found myself alongside the dark, shiny surface of the road. There were no cars then. I kneeled down and felt its rubbery, tarred texture with my hands. It was still warm, as if the heat of the cars passing over it had been sucked into it like a sponge.

It had been about three years since I'd seen a road, felt its coarseness underfoot, bent to touch it, and it seemed something wonderful to me. It was a technological wonder in an alien landscape.

From far away I heard the mechanical growl of a car approaching. I stepped back, realising what a mess I must look. With the last drops of Jonathan's water I rinsed my mouth and with a wet hand tried to clean my face. I felt the dust peeling away as I rubbed. I ran my fingers through my hair and then, figuring it was hopeless, just stood there, holding out a thumb.

But if the driver saw me, he gave no sign. The white Mercedes just sped by, leaving me to shudder like a tree in its wake. Soon after, another car passed. A third slowed down, but didn't stop. It wasn't going to be easy.

It was a large Coca-Cola truck that finally took pity on me, many passing cars later. The driver punched his horn and slowly ground his ship to a halt some fifty metres down the road.

'Come on, I don't have all night!,' he yelled as I lumbered up to the passenger door, my bloodied leg having gone numb.

I opened the door and struggled to lift myself into the seat. The man leant over and pulled me up by the arm. When I finally settled next to him, he looked at me with large eyes.

'Where on earth you coming from, mister, out here in the dead of night?' he asked. 'You look like a bladdy spook.'

'Looks worse than it is,' I said and tried to smile. 'Where you heading?'

'All the way to Joeys.'

'I'd like to go as far as you can take me, if that's okay.'

'Okay, sure-sure. I can always do with some company. Name's Themba.'

By then we were already back on the road, the headlights casting yellow beams ahead into the Karoo night, air streaming in through the open windows.

The trucker was a chubby man with a round face. Despite his short, greying hair, his body was young and muscular. 'I've picked up many hikers in my day, but never one who looked as bad as you,' he laughed. 'I don't mean to be rude. I'm just saying that you must really be down on your luck.'

'I've had a rough time of it,' I said. 'But maybe that's over now.' I tried not to look at him as I spoke. Even though it was unlikely that I would infect him in a windy cockpit like that, I couldn't be sure.

'You from around here?' he asked after a silence.

'All over, I suppose. But mostly Cape Town.'

'Ah, the Mother City,' he said. 'I have some family down there. I sometimes go by to see them when I'm down there. Strange town that, I tell you, strange. People are crazy violent down there.'

He told me how his brother-in-law, who ran a bicycle shop in Khayelitsha, had been hit once when the gangs were shooting it out in the street outside his shop. 'The bullet passed right through him. Right here,' he said and pressed a finger into the flesh next to his armpit. 'This country is falling apart, man,' he said, and looked at me, taking his eyes off the road for what felt like a full ten seconds. He was looking for a response, an answer from me, and when it wasn't forthcoming, he went on, 'And the police and the government, they don't have a clue. It is all out of control now. Out of control, I tell you. No state of emergency is going to help them this time.'

As soon as he'd said all that, he threw back his head and laughed again, completely relaxed.

I turned up the volume and we listened to Radio 2000 playing Dire Straits and some blues rock I couldn't name. There was no announcer, just an endless series of songs with little in common beyond the fact that they weren't of this century.

Ahead of us, the lights of a small town shimmered dimly in the distance. Already the horizon showed the first signs of the approaching dawn. The dark, empty wastes slid by noiselessly. I could hardly keep my eyes open.

When he reached the town, we pulled into a large filling station. A man in a BP uniform came out, and Themba clambered out, walked over to him and shook his hand. 'There are toilets over there,' Themba said, looking back at me. He pointed to a dark-green door next to a shop with a 'Closed' sign still dangling in the window. Then the two of them walked off, paying no further attention to me.

I hardly noticed the foul odour in the bathroom. I drank and drank from the tap until I felt dizzy and bloated. Then I stripped down and, using my vest and handwash from the dispenser on the wall, washed myself as best as I could at a basin. It felt wonderful to scrub the grime from my face and neck, to scoop handfuls of water onto my head and to feel the oil and dirt coming loose and be washed away.

When I was done, I dried myself as best I could with an oily towel that lay on the floor. It didn't work very well, and neither did it feel right to get back into my dirty clothes. And yet, when I stepped back into the Karoo dawn, I felt wonderful. I breathed deep, petroleum fumes and all, and felt the morning air prickle on my skin. There was something terribly vivid and real about standing there, as if I was alive again for the first time in ages. Across an intersection I could see a double-storey block of apartments where ordinary people, people untainted by disease and conscience, were no doubt still sleeping. And beyond it, a small side street disappeared between two buildings. I was amazed by the matter-of-fact reality of it all.

At the same time, that early-morning garage had something dreamlike about it, as if the clear glass of its façade reflected a new reality I hadn't really considered before. A new reality that could, of course, be shattered at any moment.

So I walked over to the truck and hung around the cab waiting for Themba.

'Hey, mister!' he called from across the tarmac. 'Come on over.' He was standing in a doorway on the other side of the shop. 'You look better,' he said when I reached him. 'This is Athol,' he nodded toward a man in a green-and-black overall and cap on a yellow plastic chair in the dimly lit room.

As I entered, the man got up and shook my hand with thin, limp fingers. He offered me coffee in a quiet, wispy voice. I accepted without a second thought. He walked over to a kettle and poured hot water into a tin cup. A small, muted black-and-white TV flashed against the wall above him. At the back of the room there was another green door, closed.

I sat listening to the two of them talking about other truckers and how expensive fuel was getting. 'They want to switch us over to electric trucks,' Themba said and laughed. 'Can you believe it? Bad publicity for Coke to be polluting the planet. But that will be even more expensive. I tell you, soon we'll all be out of a job. No one will be working.'

I sipped at the sweet coffee, grateful for the generosity of this stranger. As I drank, though, an immense hunger began to gnaw at my insides. I had no idea when I had last eaten. Nothing, I think, since the stale crusts that first night out. My mouth was watering, my stomach turned inside out at the thought of the loaf of bread that lay in a plastic bag next to the kettle. The BP man, Athol, noticed, his eyes following mine, and without a word, took two slices from the bag and handed them to me, all the time listening to Themba droning on.

I ate the bread, and it was like manna from heaven. Soft and sweet. I dipped it in the coffee. Athol smiled. 'The bakery truck dropped the bread just before you guys pulled up,' he said. 'It is for the shop, but I always take one, cost price.' He seemed smug, satisfied with himself. At the same time, a slight frown began to form on his forehead.

Themba sighed and got up. 'I'm going to the gents.' He gave Athol a conspiratorial look to which Athol faintly nodded. Then he looked at me. 'We will get going in a while, mister. You just settle down here.'

When Themba was gone, Athol and I sat looking up at the TV screen. A Bafana Bafana player missed a penalty kick and dropped to his knees in agony. It cut back to a broadly smiling newsreader. I felt Athol looking at me. He got up suddenly. A moment of indecision. Then he walked over to the door at the back of the room. He opened it and stepped out. He looked left and right. Then he came back.

'I have to go check the pumps. It is only me on duty til seven,' he said. He looked at me for a long moment. 'If you're quick, you can make it,' he said and turned away.

And then I was alone.

'So,' I thought, 'they're coming for me.'

I could hear Athol now, whistling out front. I got up from the yellow plastic chair. I limped over to the back door he had left open, the cool morning light calling me forward. With every step my knee hurt from the previous night's fall. I stopped in the doorway. There was about twenty metres of dead grass. An old Mazda was parked to the left. Beyond the grass there was a line of shacks. To the right stood some old houses, a path snaking away between them.

'This is the moment,' I told myself. 'Run. Run for your life, Barry.'

I saw myself running down that path, running like I've

never run before, disappearing amidst those old buildings and rows of shacks, finding good people to take me in, stumbling into a new way of living, fading into the reality of that settlement like dust in the desert.

But, in reality, I just stood there. I could not move. I felt the cool air on my face, the tug of clear blue air and freedom, but I remained frozen to the spot.

I heard a toilet flush. Themba. I looked back into the room.

The TV now showed a map of the Eastern Cape, a pail grey sun above it. It reminded me of the white pill.

From out front I heard the soft growl of a car pulling in to the garage, one half-whoop of a police siren. Again my heart beat faster. I looked back out across the dead grass. A wisp of smoke was rising from one of the shacks. I watched it rising. From the opposite direction came the slamming of first one car door and then another. Footsteps. A voice inside me said 'run', 'run now', but I didn't.

I just watched the dead grass, the smoke rising from that shack. Until I heard them in the room behind me, kicking away the plastic chairs, shouting. Then a firm hand on my neck pushing me forward. 'Put your hands up. Let me see your hands... Now step forward.'

I was shoved out onto the dead grass, stumbling onto my knees. There were two of them, tall policemen in dark-blue pants and light-blue shirts. They let me stand. They must have realised that I was no threat, in no condition to run away.

'Are you Barry?' the one who didn't do the shoving asked. He looked at me and then down at a crumpled page he took from the pocket of his pants. The page bore images of faces.

'Yes. I am Barry,' I said.

'Mr James Barry?'

'You could say that.'

He peered down at the paper again. 'Yes, you could be.'

'Of course it's him,' his partner interjected, still slightly out of breath. 'You'll have to come with us, Mr Barry. We're under orders to take you back... Back to Pearson. Don't even try to run again.'

He took a neatly folded mask from his shirt pocket and slid it over his face. His partner did the same. 'I'd get myself tested if I were you,' he said, looking at Themba, who had appeared from nowhere. 'These guys are infectious as hell.'

'Yes, sir,' Themba nodded, even though the two policemen were much younger than him.

'Hands,' the second policeman instructed and unhooked a pair of handcuffs from his belt. 'Your hands,' he said again when I didn't move. I looked around, and saw Themba looking away. I turned to look for Athol as well, but he was gone.

So I lifted my hands in front of me, wrists facing up, and let him slide the shackles into place. Then they led me back through the room with the yellow chairs and out to the front of the garage where Athol was checking the green-and-yellow pumps.

It was as if nothing had changed. The sun was rising in a still, cloudless sky, a car whooshed by on the road behind, I heard again in my head the thrum of Dire Straits, felt the cool wetness from the tap in the men's toilets just out of sight. I wondered what I did with Jonathan's steak knife – whether it still had blood on it. Were they really taking me back to Pearson? Did I have to leave this place already?

The less friendly of the two policemen pushed me into the back seat of the police car. He slammed the door behind me and walked over to where the other man was standing talking to Themba. Were they arguing? I didn't care if they were.

As I sat there, I looked back at the garage and the shop and the dark-green door, which the first morning light was already colouring a less distinctive shade. Soon the day's light would cut the world up, sharp as broken glass.

Then I saw that the BP man, Athol, had turned from the

pumps and stood staring toward the car. There was such a look of absentminded sadness on his thin face that I could hardly look away. I lifted my shackled hands to acknowledge him.

'Oh, Athol. Were you thinking of someone else, my brother? Your own flesh and blood, your best friend? Or is that one already dead?'

The officers climbed into the front seats, slammed their doors shut and the driver turned the ignition. It was done. 'We're taking you home where you belong, Mr Barry,' said the first policeman, turning to look back at me as the vehicle pulled away with a shudder. I looked away. The large red frame of the Coca-Cola truck still stood parked next to the garage, Themba and Athol watching as the police vehicle turned onto the road. At the corner, I knew I'd never see that truck or that garage again, nor the two men standing in the forecourt of that BP garage.

'Control, we got him,' the first policeman said into a mouthpiece. 'Mr James Barry. We're taking him straight to Pearson.'

'Copy that. I'll let them know you're coming. Please report at Pearson,' a crackly female voice offered back.

And, just like that, it was all over, this time the defeat final, not just words in a journal, my resignation an unconditional submission to fate. And yet, yet... I felt a calmness come over me as if it was all meant to be this way, as if I was meant to want the world, and also not to have it.

So we drove through the quiet early morning streets of that town. A tall red-haired man was sliding open the security gates in front of a grocery store. I imagined what it would be like in that grocery store when it opened. The sweet smell of apples, the drum of an air-conditioner starting up, a young mother rushing in for a litre of milk, a beggar, palms outstretched, asking for a single cigarette.

Two blocks further on I caught sight of a man sitting in a light-blue car, reading the paper. The windows were steamed up, cold. What was he waiting for? Was he travelling? Was he waiting for a doctor's rooms to open? Perhaps on the run from a wife who was now frantically making calls in a town three hundred kilometres back?

And then, as we turned from the main road, three large, over-dressed women walking to work, or wherever, stepped onto the pavement, absorbed in their conversation, one throwing her head back in laughter. They walked with such relaxed ease that it seemed they had been given infinity, and had thought it good.

I saw all of this, and the paper bags and milk cartons, the dry roadside gutters and the faded old poster in the window of a bottle store, and it seemed otherworldly to me, as if I was an alien just recently set down here.

On our way out of town, the houses seemed strangely exotic to me, like exhibits in a museum. With their driveways and their fences, their painted walls and dirty windows, the stubborn attempts to grow gardens in hostile terrain and in an equally hostile climate. Everything about them said that foreign men lived there, a kind of man altogether different from me.

I wanted to stop the car, climb out and walk among them. I wanted to press my face against their windows and watch these wives and husbands and children and grandparents go about their boring business. I wanted to watch them sitting down for breakfast and reading the paper. I wanted to see what odd rituals they performed in their gardens and how they passed the time in their living rooms. I wanted to know what they did with their time, what it was that made them so different from me. I wanted to penetrate that wall of nothingness that was keeping our worlds apart.

Still, I could as little reach into their world as I could go back to mine to undo my past. There was less than a stone's throw between us, but they might as well have been half a world away in a country I would never see.

Soon I had to turn in my seat in order to look back at the houses. They slipped out of sight just as they had slipped into my mind. We left town not by the N20, as Themba and I had come, but by a smaller artery that ran down toward the southwest.

The Afrikaans the two policemen spoke to each other suddenly seemed terribly strange to me. Not that I don't understand Afrikaans – I speak it quite well, in fact; it was just something about the way they spoke it, and about being there at that moment, that made it seem as foreign to me as Mandarin.

But whereas the strangeness of the town and its buildings had cast a spell on me, things were different inside the car. The policemen might have been of that other world, and might even have spoken in its strange tongues, but there was nevertheless a sickening familiarity about them, something that language could not mask.

They knew something of my empty world, and I knew something of theirs. We had strayed into the no man's land between our lives – just enough to be considered trespassing, not enough to be there legitimately.

We had hardly picked up speed when we slowed down and I saw a sign by the road that read 'Pearson'. Could it be that we had travelled a great distance in such a short time? Or, more likely, was that all Jonathan's stubbornly insistent walking had achieved, a mere twenty minute drive?

Turning off to the right, we made our way up a single-lane road that wound up an incline and when we reached the top, I saw it all laid out in front of me. There was the guard tower, the fence, and beyond it the sprawling dirty white of the hospital, so rudimentary in its simplicity that it appeared to be made of a child's building blocks.

Apart from the guard, whom I could see sitting in his tower by the gate, there was nobody else, not a soul. Two cars stood parked far off to the right, the early rays of sunlight just catching their windows. We descended slowly toward the gate. Despite all my time watching cars come up and down that road, I'd had no idea how bumpy it was. But here

I was, facing the opposite direction now, heading toward the hunchedover beast rather than away, my bones jolting as we were rattled along.

When we got to the gate, the first policeman climbed out and went up to the guardhouse. He and the guard greeted like men who knew each other, and then the guard said something into a microphone. After that, he climbed down from his tower and removed a large padlock from the gate. It used to be he could just press a button to open it, but now he flung it open with his hands.

When we passed, the guard gave me a bestubbled smile that seemed to say, 'I knew you'd be back, oh one who sits staring from the window.'

As the car swung around to park, I spotted the man introduced to us as Boesman standing at one of the outside benches. He was deep in conversation with one of the patients. He wasn't wearing the standardissue uniform of the patients, but a suit and tie. I wasn't sure if what I was seeing was real, or something conjured up by a tired, deranged mind. I looked away and made sure not to look in that direction again.

A male nurse with slicked-back black hair opened the car door as we came to a standstill. I didn't know him. Was he Dugan's replacement, I wondered. He greeted the policeman and then, turning to me, said in a nasal twang, 'Mr Barry, so glad you're back.'

'Actually, it's Mr James,' I said, 'My first name is Barry.'

'Well, okay, Barry,' he said, agitation creeping into his tone. 'Come with me; I think it will be best if you wait in one of the consultation rooms until Dr Von Hansmeyer can see you.'

I had no idea the hospital had consultation rooms, so it came as no surprise that what he led me to was little more than a small storeroom that now only contained two chairs and a table. 'I just have to help these two policemen quickly,' he said. Then he closed the door behind me and turned the key.

As soon as the door closed, the windowless room fell into pitch black. In the darkness, I walked over to the thin strip of light seeping in from under the door and groped along the walls for a light switch. I found it and flicked it on. I sat down again and waited. Eventually, tired of sitting up straight, lay down on the hard cement floor. I fell asleep with the light still on.

marginalia

ACCORDING TO RESEARCH CONDUCTED by Gumede on the authenticity of James's work, the garage could not have been a BP as indicated in the notebooks since there was no BP garage in Rietbron at the time. The only garage in town was a Total. Gumede failed to find any record of someone named Athol ever having worked at either the Total in Rietbron or the BP some distance away in Beaufort West.

Police records do, however, show that a Mr Barry James was apprehended in the town of Rietbron (precise location not given) on 4 April 2023 and taken back to the Pearson facility. There is, though, no indication that Mr James was arrested and charged. As elaborated on by Arendse, the recapture of Mr James and other escapees during this period was likely unlawful, given that government policy regarding the plague at been changed weeks before – although this official change in policy only became more widely known later. The change in policy followed a successful lawsuit in which the South African government's previous policy of forced incarceration was found to be in violation of the Constitution – a ruling that the government unsuccessfully appealed. This case is mentioned earlier in the text when James quotes Fox referring to 'upstart lawyers from Johannesburg'.

WHEN I WOKE, I had no idea where I was. I lay with my eyes closed, wondering if I might have died. But it felt like a bed beneath my back and my head seemed to be resting on a pillow, the barely perceptible weight of a sheet on my chest and legs. I thought of sniffing the air, but fearing that the effort may wake me, I decided against it.

I was filled with a familiar drowsiness, the kind you feel when just about to nod off with a smile on your face. And then, as I began to realise that I had been drugged, it dawned on me, slowly, like a bird winging over the horizon and wafting closer over a great distance, that I was back in the hospital. As the bird dropped down to perch on my outstretched arm, I remembered the journey in the police car and the black-haired nurse who had met us.

I knew that I was waking up. I wanted to linger in that prewakefulness world for a while longer, but I was pulling toward consciousness, pulled by a force that I was powerless to resist. Eventually, I could fight it no more, and let my eyelids fall open – and stared straight into the bespectacled eyes of Dr Von Hansmeyer.

At first he didn't notice that I was awake. He was staring right through me, lost in thought. Then his eyes came back into focus and met mine. 'Ah, Barry, you are awake,' he said, smiling broadly. 'We thought you had died out there, lost in the desert. You almost did die, you know.'

Only then did I notice the drip next to the bed and the large bag filled with a clear golden liquid hanging from it. I felt only a vague discomfort where the needle pierced my arm. I thought of the bird's claws digging into my forearm.

Then I opened my mouth to say something to Von Hansmeyer. He was bent over writing something in my file. But just as I wanted to say it, I forgot what it was. I still can't remember.

I was in the emergency room, in the same bed I had been in before. Someone else was lying two beds to my left. To my right the curtain was obstructing whatever was behind it. I wondered if there was another corpse there.

'What happened to your roommate?' Von Hansmeyer asked when he was done writing. 'He is one of the few we haven't found yet.'

'Jonathan?'

'Yes, Jonathan.'

Once again I saw his limp body in that shallow grave and felt the sun beating down on my back.

'I don't know,' I said. 'I lost track of him.'

He looked like he didn't believe me. 'Mmm. Well, when you are up the police will be coming to take a statement from you. So you might want to think about what you are going to tell them. There is no need to be heroic, Barry. If Jonathan killed a man, there is no reason to protect him.'

Could it be that they suspected him of Dugan's murder? The thought sent a shiver down my back. And then I clicked: Von Hansmeyer seemed to think that I had nothing to do with the murder. Did he know something I didn't?

He came round to my side and took my pulse.

'How are you feeling?' he asked, his hand moving to my forehead. I said that I was tired and that I felt like I couldn't lift my limbs. 'And your lungs? Are you breathing easily?'

I took a breath and said no. 'My lungs feel like flat tyres.'

'Inflammation. You are lucky to be alive, Barry, lucky to be alive.'

When I woke in the early evening, the bird had let go of my arm. My arms and legs felt a little lighter, but my lungs still lay like sun-baked bricks in my chest. I manoeuvred myself up on my elbows and sat up, and immediately felt the blood draining from my head. The curtains had been drawn and the only light in the room fell into it through the half-open door that led to the corridor.

I forced my legs out of bed and hovered unsteadily next to it. How had I managed to walk, and even run, less than twenty-four hours before? What unknown life force had given me the strength to keep going out there in the wilderness?

Out of the dark in front of me a voice croaked, 'Barry? It is you.'

'Morris?' I asked in the direction of the bed where I had seen someone lying before I had succumbed to the drugs and drifted off.

'Yes, it is me,' he said and waited for me to speak.

'We went looking for you. We didn't know what had happened.'

'We didn't really know ourselves. I don't know what we were thinking we'd achieve. We walked straight into it. But we needed help then. He was as good as gone.'

'Adams?'

'Yes, Adams, over there,' he said. 'Behind the curtain.'

Slowly I walked round to the curtain. The square of light that fell in through the doorway coloured the foot of the curtain a light turquoise, the standard hue of medical supplies. I stood for a moment and then pulled back the curtain.

There was no one, just an empty, unmade bed.

'He's not here,' I said.

Morris didn't answer. I climbed back into bed and lay

listening to the occasional voice drifting down the hallway toward us.

Then, after a long time, Morris cleared his throat. 'And is Jonathan not here either?'

'No,' I said. 'Jonathan got away... so to speak.'

'Ah, Jonathan... That old bastard,' he said softly, not without compassion.

We lay for a long time. Judging by how quiet the hospital was, it must have been after official lights-out. Only the echo of distant footsteps drifted in through the open door.

'So where did they pick you up?' he asked just as my thoughts were beginning to trail off.

So I told him about reaching the road and hitching a ride with a Coke truck and then being too slow to figure out that the truck driver had called the cops on me.

'They're giving out rewards, you know. That truck driver friend of yours must have thought he'd won the lottery when he picked you up.'

'At least I made someone happy.'

At this he laughed, 'Damn, you are morbid,' and for a moment I was back on the outside, on that first night out, when we'd lain on the hard earth laughing at the strange noises we make.

But if it was funny, it was in the worst possible way. Maybe we laughed because that was all that there was left to do. I guess a man can only do so much crying in his life, then his face goes hard and rubbery, the salt sets in his eyes. What sadness he has he carries with him like a bad limp.

'You know who came to see me?' Morris asked. 'Greeff. He was here this morning. He even asked about you.'

'That old man?' I could hear that Morris wanted to talk, never mind that every rough syllable required extraordinary effort on his part.

'He was good. I mean on the night we got out. Did you see that?'

'No, I was sleeping.'

'Well, he stumbles out of the front door quoting Shakespeare. Well, it sounded like Shakespeare. Anyway, he starts really quiet, and then as the guard tries to talk sense into him, he gets louder and louder. Next thing Gerrie and two nurses are out there with him. Then he shouts, "Folly, I tell you, it is folly!" I could barely stop myself from cracking up. I was in the bathroom listening through the window.'

'And then?'

'Well, he calmed down and I heard them talk a bit more before they hauled him back in. You really missed something. I don't think we could have done it without him.'

And then, quite suddenly, Morris was quiet. I waited for him to continue, but he didn't. Soon after, I heard his soft snoring, raspy and gentle at the same time, like I imagine that of a healthy man might be.

The next morning after breakfast Von Hansmeyer came round and said that I could go back to my ward. 'I trust you won't try escaping again, Barry?' he said. 'And if you do, please take some pills with you. We don't want you breeding resistance out there. As it is, we might have to change your regimen.'

It felt strange to be back in the ward without Jonathan. The beds were made and all our things had been cleared out – our clothes, our shoes, even my notebooks. I decided not to let it bother me. After all, when I left I knew I was leaving all of it behind... or did I? Either way, it was all gone now.

I lay down on the clean, neatly made bed. Everything about the ward seemed brighter, fresher, cleaner than it had ever been. Even the air, with its hint of lemon-fragranced bleach, seemed to have been purified in our absence. I had come back, but I had come back to a different place.

I turned onto my side and lay staring out the window. There it was, the hard red earth, the fence cold and glinting in the sun, the guardhouse, the road that crept up the ridge, and beyond it that great big sky. Out there nothing had changed. It was still the same indifferent world of dust and throwaway, the same merciless sun, the same fences, the same longdead god of human suffering.

I couldn't tear my eyes away from it. That I had missed it seemed crazy, but I had. I wanted to lie there forever, basking in the indifference of that all-encompassing absence out there. I wanted to let it wash over me in great big waves. I wanted to curl up and allow myself to be submerged in its weightless apathy.

As I felt myself drifting away, I noticed a car crossing the ridge. I watched it weave its way down toward the gate and park. However perfect the bubble was that had been forming around me back in this place, something seemed off kilter, out of place now.

But whether from tiredness or drugs, my eyelids couldn't stay open. What I think I remember is her walking across toward the guardhouse, handbag slung over her shoulder, a lightness to her step as if she was floating. But I could have dreamt this, because I don't remember her entering through the gate, and the image I have of her walking seems just too much like a dream.

When I finally woke, it was not to her, but to the new nurse with the slicked-back hair leaning over me and tugging on my arm. 'Mr James, the police are here to see you. Please get up.'

For a moment, I struggled to understand.

'They are waiting downstairs.'

'Okay, I'm coming,' I stuttered, and started to hoist myself out of the bed. The memory of my surroundings hit me as though I had bitten into something rotten. Every day, it seems, I wake up in a different place, somewhere else, waking into another unpredictable mess. If anything, sleep is the hole through which I fall from one unpleasant surprise to another.

They were waiting for me in the consultation room I had been held in before. The policemen weren't the same ones who had brought me in. These were clearly of another rank in that unfathomable ladder of progression in law enforcement. Two plainclothes cops with white shirts, collars and ties. One with large eyes and a small, square face, the other shorter and with a smile that reached to his ears – to go with a protruding nose, which seemed to have been twisted a few degrees off ninety, probably the result of a collapsed scrum or a bar fight by the looks of him. I wished he'd take his mask off so I could get a better look.

'When last did you see Mr Jonathan Fox?' the one with the nose asked once they had sat me down. He was seated on the other side of the metal table, while his friend with the watery eyes stood against the wall, arms folded.

'I don't know, maybe last Tuesday.'

'Very funny. We know you were amigos. We know you went out together. Now, when last did you see your friend?'

'I can't rightly say, my mind is a bit fuzzy. I think the sun might have gotten to me.'

'Okay, then… which way did you go once you got through the electric fence?'

'North,' I said.

'And who was with you?'

'Peter Pan.'

'What's your fuckin' problem?' he said. I saw his ears turning red.

The smile lines that had been visible on both sides of his mask smoothed themselves out. 'This is no joke, man. This is a murder investigation!' He slammed his fist down on the table so that its surface vibrated.

His friend just stood placidly, now and again twisting his long maroon tie around his index finger. It would have been just like in the cop shows, only there were no wires in the place, no one-way mirror, and whoever these guys were, they didn't know what they were doing.

'Now,' the one with the nose said, 'when you escaped, you broke the law. We can have you taken out of here. There are a lot worse places than this, you know. You're only being allowed to stay because the hospital is being nice – treating you like a patient rather than an escapee, a criminal.'

'What murder investigation?' I asked, pretending not to notice his anger. He buried his head in his hands and ignored me.

'One of the nurses,' the one against the wall said quietly.

'And why on earth would you suspect Jonathan?'

'We can't tell you that,' he said, looking at me with soft eyes that seemed to want to assure me that everything would be fine. His large-nosed friend snorted and swore under his breath.

'Jonathan is not your man,' I said.

'Okay,' Soft Eyes said. 'Then help us find the real killer.'

I explained that Jonathan had woken me up and that when we got downstairs Dugan was already lying in a puddle of his own blood. 'Jonathan was as shocked as I was.' I figured I might as well lie since they wouldn't believe me anyway.

'I thought you didn't know that someone got killed,' interjected The Nose, his head shooting up, his eyes bloodshot.

'I must have forgotten,' I said.

'You, you are digging a grave for yourself, mister,' he said.

'And outside, where and when did you last see him? Fox, I mean…' Soft Eyes asked, placing a restraining hand on his partner's shoulder. And there we were, exactly where I didn't want to be. I had no idea whether Morris had talked to them yet. Did they know that we had all been travelling together? Did Morris spill the beans about the ruined old house?

'I lost track of Jonathan when we were out,' I said after making them wait a little. 'I figured my best chance would be to keep going north to the N20. I didn't want to walk into a roadblock. Jonathan didn't care – he was going straight east, he said. What can I say? He was right, I was wrong.'

'Are you sure you are not lying to us?' The Nose said, looking at me with what must have been a mix of resentment and suspicion. Even so, I thought they bought it.

'That's about as honest as I can be,' I said.

'So, you travelled alone? Is that your official statement?'

'Yes, alone.'

When they let me go, I went to see Morris. He was alone

in the quiet of the emergency room. He lay snoring that same soft, pleasant snore, that of someone at peace with the world, the kind of snore you'd expect from a man nodding off in his own lounge while watching television.

I sat at his bedside and waited for him to wake. A nurse came in, took a sceptical look at us and turned around again. Eventually the bell ran for lunch. I wasn't very hungry, but I went to the dining hall anyway. Maybe I shouldn't have.

I passed the spot where Dugan's body had lain. There was a tray table standing there, as if nothing had happened. I stood in line for some of the rice and watery stew, and as I waited, I realised how empty the hall was. Then I wondered where I was going to sit. The three I always sat with were all gone – Jonathan rotting in the Karoo sand, Morris snoring peacefully in the emergency room, Adams probably frozen in the morgue. Like Jonathan, he was sleeping the big sleep.

In the end, I sat on my own and struggled to get through even half the food on my plate.

Afterwards, back in emergency, I found Morris sitting up with a tray on his lap. I told him about the morning's interrogation. He assured me I had nothing to worry about, that the police hadn't spoken to him yet.

'If they ask me,' said, 'I'll say that Adams and I were on our own.'

'Thank you. That should keep them off my back.'

'No problem, suits me fine. I couldn't care less what really happened.' Back in my ward, I lay down again. I felt weaker than ever. Von Hansmeyer suspected I had done irreparable damage to my lungs during the escape, those long cold nights in the Karoo, the hot dry days. And I could feel it. It felt like I was breathing into a deflated football; no matter how much I tried, I couldn't get it to inflate, even a little. A crumpled-up mess of inflamed scar tissue that wouldn't budge.

So I breathed my shallow breaths and waited. For what, I didn't know or didn't much care.

The ward seemed strangely empty without Jonathan. In

fact, the whole hospital seemed empty to me. The dining hall, the corridors, the bathrooms, and the yard, it all felt deserted, as if those of us who still lingered had come to school during the holidays.

The following day I would mention this to Morris on his return to the dining hall, and he'd tell me that a nurse had told him that the hospital wasn't taking in any new patients, that there would be no further intakes. Apparently, the premier had stepped in and shut things down after the escape.

As I would later read in the paper, a Human Sciences Research Council study had found that there were at least ten times as many infected people as there was room in all the country's quarantine facilities combined. Maybe that was why we weren't taking in new patients. According to the paper, the new buzzword was community-based treatment. The way I understand it, patients were staying at home and getting their meds delivered to them by specially trained health workers. There was also some new kind of mask these patients had to wear whenever they were around people not infected – or not yet infected, anyway.

It all sounded a little like quitting to me. The great quarantine experiment abandoned at long last. But, for all of that, it meant little to us here of course. Obviously, they couldn't just let us go. Those already inside quarantine facilities had to wait it out. Maybe they thought it would be bad press to have front-page images of those infected being released, to spend their last days among the healthy and the happy. Besides, apart from all the studies and all the calls for change, government policy was still officially to keep everyone locked up.

I didn't know any of this that afternoon, though. All I knew was that the hospital seemed empty to me; that out at the gate there was very little activity. There weren't any Department of Health minibuses dropping off new patients. The comings and goings of the staff seemed to have slowed to a crawl.

Even the guard in his cubicle at the gate was sitting with his chin in his hands.

All there really was was the sun, as relentless as ever, and a stifling breeze playing a lonely game with handfuls of dust. I lay watching until the shadows shifted and the breeze gathered strength and started tossing around much larger scoops of the dry redness.

I slept a dreamless sleep through dinner and well into the night. At some point I was woken for my meds: a pill stuck between my lips, my head raised from the pillow and a glug of water. But I could have imagined it. The lines between the sleeping and waking life remained fuzzy.

As soon as I opened my mouth to speak, I knew that our meeting again had been inevitable. It was out in the back yard. I had gone out late one afternoon to sit in the shade, my back against the wall of the laundry rooms when it happened.

I saw her coming out of the main building. A black dress and black stockings. I smiled at her, and she walked over. She stopped in front of me and looked straight into my eyes.

'I'm very unhappy with you Barry,' she said, her voice dry. She cleared her throat and looked as if she was going to turn away.

'Please sit down,' I said. She hesitated, but to my surprise, she did. We looked out over the yard, the shadows of the buildings stretching ever longer. Two men were chatting on a bench. It was not too hot or too cold. It was almost idyllic.

'Okay then. How are you, Barry?' she asked.

I couldn't help but smile. 'I'm okay,' I said. 'I've had a rough ride, but I'm okay.'

'I am quite mad at you Barry. I wasn't sure you'd be coming back.'

'I always knew I'd be back. I might even have gotten myself caught on purpose. I don't know.'

'I missed you,' she said in a voice that was barely audible. 'What if you had died out there?'

'I think I missed you too.'

She looked at me with a sad look in her eyes that I hadn't seen before.

I was frightened. Something was wrong. 'Yes,' she said without thinking. It was as if something had snapped in her voice, as if what gave her substance had melted away since I had last seen her.

'This is the spot where Espoir and Kagiso had their big fight,' I said after a while. 'Were you here then?'

'No, but I heard about it.'

'They wrestled each other right here. I'm surprised there aren't any bloodstains. It was one of the saddest things I've ever seen.'

'Barry, I'm going away in a few weeks' time. I have resigned my post in town and am ending my contract here at the hospital.'

'Okay...' was all I could manage. Not sure whether she expected more.

'Something happened a while back... Something bad,' she said and gently bit her lip. She sighed quietly and folded her arms. I felt a shiver pass through my whole body.

'It could have been much worse, I suppose,' she said, staring toward the fence. 'Still, I don't feel I can talk about it. I'm sorry – you told me everything, and now I'm holding back.'

'It's okay,' I said. 'You don't have to talk.'

She said nothing more about it, but I knew from the tone of her voice that her faith in the world or in people had been shaken, and for the first time in years I felt like crying. I had to stop my mind from imagining it. Had she been robbed? Had some thug attacked her, or worse, had she been raped? I tried to banish the word from my mind.

She said she had applied for a British visa. 'It is the one

good thing about being a psychologist, the whole world wants you.'

'I'm sorry,' I said.

'Yes,' she said, absent-mindedly tracing a line through the red dust on the grey cement with her index finger.

When we got up, she dusted herself off and tucked a wisp of hair behind her ear. She would come again the next day if I wanted, she said. 'I'd like to hear what happened to you... if you want to tell me, of course.'

'Okay, tomorrow's good,' I said. 'I don't think I have any appointments.'

She smiled half-heartedly at my joke and I was glad for making it.

I wondered if I should ask about what had happened to her, but I didn't feel I could.

THAT NIGHT, I COUGHED blood again. It wasn't as bad as it had been before, but I was alone in the ward, so there was no one to notice. The blood was choking me. I wanted to call out, to scream, but I couldn't. I thought of banging the plastic cup on my bedside drawer against the metal frame of the bed to attract attention. Before I could get that far, it was over. My throat was open enough for me to scream, so I screamed.

When a nurse flicked on the light, I was shocked to see so much blood. A large, red puddle spread across the white sheet and slowly dripped to the floor. It was already darkening in colour. The nurse jabbed me in the arm with something, and soon I felt that old familiar friend driving me away in his fine black chariot. Swing low, we are going to the ballroom tonight.

In keeping with my life of strange awakenings, I woke mid-morning in the emergency room, not sure whether I had dreamt the last few days. Had the police interrogation really happened? And the talk with Morris and Ms Van Vuuren? It could very well have been a dream, my drugged-up imagination grasping at vestiges of reality that always remained elusive. If you live your life in such small confines, one day quickly becomes like another and the patterns can easily run ragged. Who knows what happened when and, in the end, who cares?

Listening to me breathe through his stethoscope, Von Hansmeyer said that the news wasn't good. 'Lungs do not recover from this condition,' he said. Then he made me cough him up a sputum sample. Why he wanted it if he was so sure, I didn't know.

'You may have more of these events now, Barry,' he said. 'There is nothing we can do about it.' He asked me if I was in any pain – I lied, of course – and promptly gave me another injection.

'Okay, Barry, you need to take Vintramol once a day as before. It is not how I would have wanted it, but the department is not sending us any more Ephedrine.'

'Why not, Doc?'

'No leadership, Barry, no leadership. They pretend there is no money.' As I felt the drug starting to take effect, I remembered the premier and his convoy as they stood parked out beyond the fence just a few months ago. And now that man was being mentioned as a possible candidate for president.

She did come to see me that day, just as she had done once, many months before, also in the emergency room. I was awake when she came in. She had radiating about her that spicy perfume now so familiar. She pulled up a chair and sat down next to the bed, her eyes much clearer than the day before.

'How are you?' she asked.

'I'll live, for a bit.'

It wasn't too serious, I said. I had progressed to some late-stage condition, which was bad, but at least it wasn't like the time I had the nodular rupture. She asked if I felt up to talking and I said I did. I figured it would be crazy to let her go again.

'Anything specific on your mind?' she asked.

'My mind's like a sieve, things just flow through it.'

'Nothing sticking then?'

'I think of Jonathan sometimes,' I admitted. I didn't know how much I should tell her, so I didn't say anything more.

'The police asked me about him – and about you,' she said. 'They wanted to know if you were good friends. I didn't really know him, so I couldn't really tell them much. Come to think of it, I only saw the two of you together that once.'

'When he waved at you from down in the yard?'

'Yes.'

'Yeah, well, that's all over now...' I thought of his boyish old body in that sandy grave.

'I think they'll keep looking for him. It was in all the papers. What happened here that night. What happened to Dugan. They really made your friend sound like a monster.'

'I wish they'd just let him be,' I said. 'He wasn't like that at all.'

'Barry, I'm not supposed to tell you this, but they found his fingerprints on the murder weapon. They are quite sure he did it.'

'Doesn't make sense,' I said. And then I didn't know what else to say.

I wanted to ask about Kagiso and Sibu. Did they ever find them? But all I could manage was, 'I don't think he did it.'

'Maybe you are right,' she said and remained silent for a long time. She kept looking at me, though, her eyes wide and clear.

'Doesn't really matter anyway, does it?' I said. 'Soon the hospital won't be here any more. Give it some time and no one will give a second thought to what happened to Jonathan Fox.'

'You may be right.'

'They're going to shut the hospital down. The world's falling to pieces. Floods and droughts everywhere. I'm not even sure you'll be safe in England.'

'Oh, Barry, you can be so gloomy sometimes.' Something about the way she said it made me think she wasn't all that optimistic either. But perhaps I was wrong, maybe it was just my own mind clouding things over again.

'I'm more worried about what's going to happen to you,' she said. 'Don't worry, I'll be okay. I'm not afraid of anything any more.'

'And the past?' she asked, her voice soft again, as it always was when she thought she was asking a serious question.

'That... I don't know.' I caught myself sighing. 'All that's kind of faded since the escape. Maybe we escaped from the past, lost it like you lose a police car chasing you in the movies.'

'Barry, you only get to escape when you get really old and develop dementia,' she said.

I didn't know what to say. I figured out too late that she meant it as a joke.

'Okay then, I have to get going,' she said. 'I can't come tomorrow, but maybe the next day.' Then, as she got up to leave, she touched my forearm with her fingertips, gently, so gently that I almost wasn't sure it had really happened.

Either way, it was enough.

I MOVED BACK TO the ward the next morning. That doesn't mean I felt any better. I knew that I had turned a corner, that my body had given me a signal and that the finishing line was near. I don't know how I knew this, but it seemed obvious to me. I had turned off the main road onto a quiet street in some industrial area. Soon I'd have to knock at the door of some warehouse, where an electric door would open and then slam shut behind me, never to open again. Anyway, that is how I saw it as I lay on my bed that morning, drifting in and out of sleep. It wasn't a sad or depressing thought, just a fact, a given, a part of the script I knew I would have to play out.

A nurse checked up on me and got me to go downstairs for lunch. I ate only a few bites of the mushy, grey slop they dished up for us. I sat with Morris, but we didn't speak. When I left, I told him, 'See you later.' He just grunted and lifted his knife a little to acknowledge my leaving.

I could hardly make it back upstairs, the synapses in my nerves refusing to cooperate. It seemed my muscles had stopped obeying my brain. They seemed stiff and unwieldy, as if already half dead. Still, even though I was tired as hell – they had given me more pills – I didn't want to go back to sleep. All the lying about of the morning had given me a headache that was lingering like a dark, menacing shape in the corner of my eye. I knew that as soon as I lay down, it would pounce.

So I pulled up the chair and sat staring out my ward window like I had done so many times before. Outside, the sun was pounding the wasteland with such a brightness as I had not seen for some time.

I sat and looked at the pale, cloudless dome that covered the earth and not for the first time I was struck by just how empty it was. I considered opening the window, but I knew it would be too hot out there beyond the windowpane. From the feeble way in which the wind shouldered the waning leaves of the remaining throwaway, I knew it would offer no respite.

My eyelids dropping dark curtains over the burning veld, I thought of my conversation with Ms Van Vuuren the previous day. That, too, seemed as if it had happened in a long-ago dream. But it hadn't been a dream. It had been as real as any interaction as any could be. And she did touch my arm, however little or how much that might have meant. Does it matter if reality sometimes seems like a dream?

When I opened my eyes minutes later, slightly dazed and with a yawn welling up in me, I spotted a white speck making its way over the sunstroked horizon and slowly start slipping down the ridge. I watched for a moment, just a wavy spec moving down almost imperceptibly. My heart beat a little faster, though my eyelids remained heavy.

She's only coming tomorrow, I thought. Surely it can't be her. You must be dreaming. And then the yawn that had been threatening overpowered me. I wondered whether I was yawning more now that my body's ability to absorb oxygen was diminishing.

I looked back out at the white speck. Then, as it wound down the slope, a sudden coldness pass over me like an electric shock. I was wide awake and confused. It was not a Hyundai, but a Corolla, and I knew immediately that I'd seen it before.

In the front seat, a man sat up very straight, his shirt an

immaculate white. Next to him sat a much smaller figure, hardly visible due to the angle of the light. They were about a hundred metres from the gate. I couldn't really be certain yet; it didn't make sense after all. It could just be the heat, I thought. One of those weird hallucinations brought on by heat stroke. Had I been out walking that morning? Had I taken too many pills? Surely it couldn't be. Surely…

I closed my eyes. In the ward, too, it was getting hot. I wondered if they'd be gone when I looked again, wiped away like the distant memories of a dream. Please, God, I whispered. I wiped my forehead. It was drenched. But when I opened my eyes, the world wasn't reconfigured; it was all exactly the same, except that it had turned wet and glassy.

I felt a vine clawing at my throat as the car stopped and the man stepped out, stretching his arms and looking about him. His large forehead was unmistakable. He leant down to the car window and said something to the passenger. The light was still dancing on the windscreen, obscuring her identity but, even without seeing her, I knew it was a woman. Then he got up and stood looking at the building, his shirt now a white blur in my muddled vision. I felt my jaw tighten. Damn you, mama's boy, damn you!

When I looked again, Sarah was closing the car door behind her… a girl in a light-blue dress, a girl with sandy hair, a girl I had once known. Together they walked over to the guardhouse. How small and stocky she now seemed next to him. How unlike the girl I had kept alive in my memories.

No, no, no. It cannot be. She was dead. There had been a funeral. It had been in the paper. All of it was impossible. The universe doesn't just change like that… There was a fucking current that took me away from all this.

But of course I knew… I knew all along, and that is why something cracked inside me, maybe the last time anything would ever crack inside me.

When the dark-haired nurse eventually came into my room to say in his nasal twang that I had visitors, I told him to leave.

'I don't want to see them. Tell them to go away. Tell them I'm too sick. Tell them they do not belong here. Tell them to go back to Neverland.'

He just stood there. 'But Mr Barry…'

'Go! Fuck!' I shouted at him. 'I don't want to see them! I have a right to decide who I see and who I don't. You are not going to change my mind.' Slowly, he turned and left, looking back at me one last time with a look that said, you're crazy.

To the idiot's credit, though, he did get rid of them. Not that I remembered looking out of the window to watch them go, snake their way back up the ridge – in fact, I actually have no recollection of what happened to the rest of the afternoon. It disappeared, like things disappear when you drink too much cheap whisky and then drink some more.

I guess I just stayed in the ward. Maybe I buried my head under my pillow. Maybe I screamed like an angry child. Maybe I was paralysed with shock, or maybe I went about my business like any other afternoon. I just don't know. The memory has slipped my mind.

What I do remember, though, is looking out of the window much, much later and being surprised to find them gone. The dusky air out there was scattered with clouds of red dust. The wind had picked up and the wastes seemed even emptier than before. Everything was quiet, dead quiet.

Later that night I thought I heard Ms Van Vuuren's voice saying, 'Maybe they were never here.' It sounded so real that I was startled and sat up to check whether she was there, in the ward, seated next to my bed. But of course she was not. It was just me in an empty ward, in a decaying hospital, in a mad country, on an over-heated planet, losing my mind.

THE NEXT DAY I didn't get up for breakfast. I just lay there, slumped in a stupor, as if I was one of those drooling, lobotomised automatons you find in bona fide asylums. In a brief moment of clarity, it crossed my mind that my soul had finally descended to those cavernous doldrums where my body had been drifting about for so long.

I'd probably have stayed like that all day had Von Hansmeyer not burst in, booming, 'Good afternoon, Barry!' He flung open the windows and instructed me to get up and to get dressed. I couldn't have cared less, so I ignored him. 'Come on,' he said, standing next to my bed with his hands on his hips. 'Ms Van Vuuren is waiting for you.'

'I want one of those pills you gave me,' I said.

'Which pills?'

'The white ones. That big one you gave me… that day I was in your office.'

'Oh, those…,' he said and turned around to leave. 'She – Van Vuuren – is waiting for you. Don't make the nice lady wait.'

He just assumed I'd obey, and, as always, the old German was right. So I got up on autopilot, the thought flashing through my mind that, at least, there could not be much of this 'getting up business' left to do. The way things just went on and on suddenly made me feel terribly tired.

I washed my face and was surprised at how familiar the face in the mirror looked to me. It might have gotten thinner and a little sunburnt, and it hadn't had a decent shave in months, but the lines were still the same. For all that had happened, it was still the same guy looking back at me as ten years before. It seemed inappropriate somehow.

She was writing something in a file when I tapped on the door. Behind her the window let in a soft breeze. It had cooled down substantially since the previous day. I sat down, and something in her eyes told me that she was smiling at me from behind her mask. She said hello and I nodded back at her.

'I heard you had some visitors yesterday, Barry,' she said.

'Did I?'

'Yes, so I was told. And I take it you weren't very happy to see them.'

I didn't say anything.

'It was Sarah, wasn't it?'

I dropped my head into my hands.

'I was afraid of that,' she said quietly.

We sat in silence like that for a long time. She scribbled something on the page in front of her. I just sat there, not thinking.

'I brought these for you,' she said and took out a pile of notebooks from her handbag. 'I saw them in Von Hansmeyer's office after you ran off and thought I'd better hang on to them, keep them for you. There are also some new ones, if you want them.'

'Did you read them?'

'Yes, I did,' she said, lowering her eyes. 'But that was before I knew you were back though.'

'That's okay,' I said. 'I don't really mind.'

She shoved the pile of books over to my side of the desk. Then she took out a pack of four brand-new black pencils and handed that over as well.

'After all that, you're still encouraging me?'

'So, do you know how you got infected?' she asked.

'Which version do you want?' When she didn't answer, I went on, 'There is really no way of knowing. Hell knows, it could have been anywhere. Maybe on the train – I used to take the train to work.'

'It's so random, isn't it?'

'I suppose.'

'I'm sorry this happened to you, Barry. You really didn't deserve this. You just had some very, very bad luck.'

'It's okay, you don't have to be sorry.'

'At least Sarah is still alive,' she said, and she was right.

For some reason, just then, I thought of Jonathan lying in his shallow grave. I wanted to tell her. I couldn't, though. I knew that she would have to tell Von Hansmeyer or the police, and that they would then go out there to dig him up. No, that was not going to happen.

'Yes, I suppose Sarah is still out there.'

'As you knew all along,' she said, as if slowly putting together the extent of my lies, my delusions.

'Yes, you could say I knew.'

'And you're sure you don't want to see her again?'

I thought of how I could explain that Sarah and I occupied different worlds, that we'd pass by each other the way ghosts pass the living. 'Maybe you think I'm going mad. I don't know. Maybe things happen to you when you are locked up in a place like this. Maybe you lose your mind… Who knows? But I think that when you're halfway to the other side and you get to look back like I did, maybe you see things in their rightful place, in ways you can't when you're out there in the real world.'

'But the past,' she said, 'I mean the past as it really was, surely some of that is worth holding on to?'

'There is no past *as it really was*, as you put it. That past is dead. Do you really want me to give you the straight story…? You want to hear that it was all a lie? That I was just an ordinary guy in a dead-end job when I got sick for absolutely no reason? That Sarah was never my girlfriend? That she certainly wouldn't let me sleep with her, let alone make her pregnant? That I made it all up?'

I could feel my voice giving way. I fully expected her to say yes, she does, but she didn't. She just sat there and looked at me as if she was trying to understand something with her eyes.

'I think I understand,' she said eventually. How much she understood, I didn't know. That I'd managed to put any kind of explanation to things had come as a surprise to me. I wasn't sure any of it made sense. At least it felt like understanding, even if it was shot through with holes.

'All of this is not punishment then,' she said softly.

'No, I guess not. I guess I'm not that lucky. I guess there is no sense to it. It just is what it is.'

'I'm so sorry, Barry,' she said, and I thought for a moment that she was going to cry.

That was the last time I saw Ms Van Vuuren. I walked her down and at the front door she said that she'd try to come again in two or three days' time. That never happened. I watched her walking off toward her car, slipping the mask off her face and dangling it from her hand as she walked. I turned to go back into the building.

Back in the ward, I took one of the new notebooks from the pile she had given me and started writing.

It was over the next few days that the patients started dropping like flies in a snowstorm. There was an outbreak of an unknown opportunistic infection they couldn't trace. We were told not to gather in the dining hall, and then not to visit each other's wards. I think they suspected the water supply, but they couldn't tell us not to drink, and they sure as hell weren't going to buy us bottled water. They boiled large urns of water and left them in the dining hall where we could come and fill bottles they had given us. It didn't help. People still succumbed. They still died. One after the other.

Sitting at my ward window, I watched them loading bodies

into ambulances and taking them away. Whatever it was, I seemed to be immune. That doesn't mean I wasn't sick, though. I was growing weaker and weaker by the day.

Then one morning, a few days later, a nurse dropped a letter in my room. It was from Ms Van Vuuren. She said that she was sorry she didn't get to see me again. 'As you read this,' she wrote, 'I'll probably be on my way to Pretoria. I have to finalise my arrangements from there. If everything goes according to plan, I shall be leaving for London within weeks.'

She gave me the address of a place in Richmond where she would be staying. 'In case you want to write to me,' she said. I felt strangely touched by this courtesy. After all, if anything, I was in the first instance a patient rather than a friend, or a potential penpal. Sure, she knew that I wouldn't harass her with letters, or turn up in London knocking on her door looking for a place to stay, but still, the gesture moved me deeply.

To be honest, I also felt a sense of relief. For days I had been scanning the ridge, waiting for her to come back. Knowing that she wouldn't be coming felt like loss – loss that wrenched and gnawed at my gut – but at least I could stop waiting.

I wrote more and more… as I am writing now. For whom, I cannot say. Whenever I felt strong enough, I would get up and put pen to paper.

I hardly spoke to anyone. Besides, there was hardly anyone left to talk to.

Morris did come to see me one last time. He told me about how the police had quizzed him about Jonathan, and how he had told them that he and Adams had travelled alone. They had had no trouble believing him. He had that kind of face. I didn't tell him about the fingerprints. Like a lot of other things, it no longer mattered. None of it did.

After a while, Morris and I didn't know what to say to each other. We didn't have much more in common than our shared past, brief as it was, and neither of us felt much like talking about that. In reality, he had been friends with Adams and Jonathan – I just happened to be there as well. No matter.

Then, one morning, as I looked out the ward window, I saw that the massive iron gates were open. They just stood there, abandoned, already the look of disuse about them. There was no one in the guardhouse.

I went out into the corridor and found one of the patients – a tall, thin guy whose name I forget – coming out of the bathroom. I asked him what was up and he said that the hospital was closing down and that they were moving us to another. He was matter-of-fact, his eyes emotionless, like it had been inevitable, that he'd seen it coming.

I grabbed hold of Von Hansmeyer as he came rushing up the stairs. 'Excuse me, Doctor, what's this about closing down?'

'Yes, you must get ready, Barry – the buses are coming for you at three this afternoon,' he said without slowing down.

I trailed him to his office. When I eventually caught up with him, he was standing at his desk, packing papers into a cardboard box.

'Yes, Barry?' he said without looking up.

'That white pill–' I started saying, but he cut me off before I could finish.

'Ah, Barry, that was a placebo,' he said, continuing to rummage in his desk. 'Just a placebo. One left from a trial we did years ago. Now off you go – get yourself ready.'

Later, when I saw the Department of Health minibuses pulling in through the open gate, I realised that if I wanted to stay I would need supplies. So I once again struggled down the stairs. In the kitchen I found boxes with unopened packs of rice, bread, and other foodstuff packed out on the stainless-steel counters. There was no one there, so I helped myself: four loaves of bread, a large can of apricot jam. I packed all of it into one of the small boxes that stood at the ready, to be packed and despatched as part of the great evacuation, and made my way back to the wards. In all the commotion, no one gave me a second look.

I holed up in a cupboard in a storeroom at the furthest end of the hospital, a wing long since cleared out and abandoned, even before patient numbers had started to dwindle, when staff cuts meant the hospital had had to tighten its belt, spread the meagre resources more efficiently.

After what must have been at least four or five hours, I finally ventured back out. I knew immediately that they were all gone. Apart from the distant sounds of coughing, the hospital had always been a quiet place. Now, however, it was deathly quiet. The evacuation had been quick and thorough. There were still beds and linen in the wards, but all life had been extracted. I was a walking corpse inside a rotting carcass. In time, they would no doubt be back for the beds and whatever else may be salvageable, I thought, but for now the place had been all but abandoned. Forgotten.

The echoing corridors were eerily dark. I felt around along the wall of a ward I didn't know and found the light switch. It didn't work, and neither did any of the others. All the windows had been closed, the heat that had built up during the day cloying at my bones. So I went to my ward, lay down on my bed, the windows thrown open wide to allow the coolness of the night to seep in. I was utterly alone.

That night I again heard the small orchestra playing in the ballroom. As before, I was wearing the same ill-fitting suit. I was standing by the window on the landing by the stairs. Outside, the world was covered with snow.

Then I was in the ballroom, and this time it was full of people. Kagiso was in a finely tailored suit, a drink in hand, talking to Adams. Dugan winked at me as he led an unfamiliar girl with long black hair onto the dancefloor. I saw Von Hansmeyer poking by a fire in the giant grate. On the balcony, the man playing the violin made me think of the poet Virgil.

As I once again stood by the large window that looked out on the snow and woods beyond, I heard Ms van Vuuren saying 'Barry?' next to me.

'But you've gone to Pretoria,' I said.

'Well, I'm here,' she said. As before, she was dressed all in white, her shoulders bare, and gloves up to her elbows, her lips red, her hair tied back. I looked down at my own ill-fitting suit, and she said it's okay. 'It doesn't matter.'

She offered me her hand and I remember being scared that I wouldn't be able to move, that the lethargy of dreams, the moving as if stuck in sand, would take hold of me. But it didn't.

From the balcony, a Balkan waltz filled the ballroom with a sweeping melody, every now and again flirting at the edge of madness and dissonance. She and I danced, and it was intoxicating. And as we rose and fell, I saw that all those around us were also dancing, and that, like me, their clothes didn't fit them and that their bodies seemed weak, that some had injuries, and that there was even a trickle of blood from Dugan's neck.

None of the pain mattered. We danced, and it was as if all the world had fallen from us like dirt, as if the ballroom itself was about to take off and blur the snowy landscape outside the window into an indistinguishable mess.

When I woke, I felt a sense of joy inside me. I knew that as long as I could hang on to that dream, I could bask in that warm glow. So I wrote it down, as I wrote down all the others.

All that day, I was alone. When I felt strong enough, I wrote in the notebooks. The rest of the time I just sat staring out at the ridge. No one came. It was just the open gate and the red dust being blown about, ever so gently.

When I felt strong, I walked around in the empty hospital. I opened windows here and there. Already the air was getting stale. I didn't bother closing any of the windows behind me. In fact, I felt a strange sense of satisfaction when coming across a room where I had been earlier, and finding the floors covered in a thin layer of fine dust. There, amid the dust, I found a kind of peace.

At night the hospital was very dark. I moved my chair as close to the window as I could and looked at the stars. I once went looking for candles, but I didn't look very hard or for very long. The darkness suited me fine.

By the third day, I opened a tap and there was nothing. I tried other taps and they too were empty. The game was up. It didn't upset or surprise me. I had expected it and it seemed as ordinary as the rest of my dream world.

THIS MORNING, AS THE sun climbs to its zenith, I look out of my ward window one last time. The open gates still seem strange to me, but I like them being open. It's as if a painting I've been looking at for years has been changed. I didn't like the change at first, but I've come around to it. Once we had a locked gate keeping people in, now we have an open gate no one passes through. I like it more and more.

I stand for a long minute facing the ward window one last time. I leave the notebooks behind on the bedside drawer and trudge down the echoing stairs. The front door is locked. I rattle the knob. I give it a kick, but it doesn't budge.

'Let it be,' I say out loud.

So I open a window and climb out into the sweltering day.

When I get to the gates, I stand still in that space that had been closed for so long. I try to sense something of the openness around me. I try to feel some significance, but I feel no elation, no sense of fulfilment, nothing. Around me, the silence is complete. The sun burns into my neck and down on my head. I look back at the empty hospital just one more time before I start climbing the ridge.

I do not look back when I reach the top. I don't even look sideways. I just walk on down to the road. Already the heat is shrinking the world around me, closing down possibilities. The fabric of things is caving in around me, folding all existence down to a narrow tunnel.

When I reach the road, I can feel the tar burning through the soles of my shoes. But I ignore it. I ignore it all. I turn to the right and start off down the road.

I trudge on. It is hard to tell how long I have been on this road or how far I've come. Eventually, from the corners of my vision, the world starts closing in, the outline of shapes and forms blurring, taking on a shade of reddish black, until finally it fills all in front of me. My knees melt away slowly, giving way like soft, pliable metal.

I do not notice hitting the ground. All I know is that I am lying on my back. Beneath me the road is searing, as though it is burning. Lying here, I feel my lungs filling with something thick and glue-like. I want to cough. I know I should cough, but I cannot. My body simply doesn't respond anymore.

As I lie waiting, I hear a soft whirring sound, and a rush of terror shoots through me like a final convulsion. The whirring is getting louder and louder. I know it is the car from my nightmare, the car with the blue plastic round its wheels. It gets even louder and louder, and then it is next to me. It stops. A car door opens and slams shut. I open my eyes, and against the pale, radiated sky, I see a man bending down over me, a long scar down the side of his face.

'It's okay,' he tells me. 'Don't worry. There is nothing to be afraid of. There is nothing on the other side.' And as he says this it is as if a great load is lifted. I know that I am dying, and finally, I am glad for the cold indifference of it.

editor's note

THE FINAL SECTION, WRITTEN in the first person present tense, is all there is in the eighth notebook. Whereas it is tempting to believe that Mr James had written his own death, his body was never found. If he had died on the old Rietbron road as the fragment suggests, his body would almost certainly have been found and the case would have been indicated in official police records. There is no record of Mr James's whereabouts or death.

It does, however, seem likely that he was not evacuated along with the other patients at Pearson, since there is no record of him in the registers kept at the Beaufort West camp where patients were taken after the evacuation from Pearson.

acknowledgements

THANK YOU TO MY literary agent, Aoife Lennon-Ritchie, for her belief in the book and her unwavering encouragement. Aoife resurrected this novel at a time when I had given up on it. Thank you also to Henrietta Rose-Innes for her sagely guidance in the initial writing of *Asylum* and for encouraging me to get it published. Thank you to Mariette Olwagen, who gave her time freely to edit an earlier version of the book. Thank you to my truly excellent editor, Sean Fraser, for helping me make the novel better than it was before, and to Russell Stark for his brilliant cover design. Thank you also to Andrea Nattrass and Terry Morris at Pan Macmillan South Africa for believing in *Asylum*.

On a more personal level, I thank Marie and Otto Low for the years of unconditional support and encouragement. So many people have been good and kind to me along the way – I wish I had room here to thank each of you.

Finally, some of the most important friends and mentors in my writing life have passed away in recent years. Mariana Steyl, more than any other person, opened my eyes to the world of books. Jaco Botha, in the kindest way possible, dispelled much of my youthful naivety about writing and introduced me to Raymond Carver. Stephen Watson was a friend and ally at a critical time. I miss and thank all three of them.

If you enjoyed what you read, don't keep it
a secret.

Review the book online and tell anyone
who will listen.

Thanks for your support spreading the word
about Legend Press!

Follow us on Twitter

@legend_press

Follow us on Instagram

@legendpress